A DE

"Only proof I have is my word," Cole said. "The men who did the hanging took the horses."

Rudolpho's eyes fixed Cole hard. "Senor, I think you are a liar. You are the killer, no?"

"No," Cole repeated flatly.

Everything was quiet. Tense. Somebody was going to die. A child wailed. People drew back uneasily.

"These men, which way did they go?" Rudolpho asked.

Cole knew the Mexican was stalling, waiting for the right moment.

"That way," Cole said, merely nodding his head to the east, keeping his eyes fastened on Rudolpho.

Rudolpho's gun hand was poised, his left holding the quirt alongside his leg.

Cole knew the idle talk was over.

Each man stared at the other, neither man blinking, each man waiting for the other to make a play.

A DEADLY ACCUSATION

HIGH PRAIRIE

HIRAM KING

LEISURE BOOKS   NEW YORK CITY

To my wife, Grace, a longtime
trail partner
and
My granddaughters Danielle Rene
and Alexis Laverne

A LEISURE BOOK®

November 1997

Published by

Dorchester Publishing Co., Inc.
276 Fifth Avenue
New York, NY 10001

ISBN 0-8439-4324-6

HIGH PRAIRIE

Chapter One

That town down there meant trouble and he knew it. He sat his buckskin horse in the runoff notch on top of the craggy bluff, looking down on the raw settlement. He was a black man, tall, rangy, twenty-three years old. He had on faded jeans, a pair of wide Mexican shotgun chaps made of rough leather, and a checked black shirt, now stiff with sweat and the dust of the trail. His boots were scruffy, down-at-the-heels. A pistol was belted around his waist, a sixteen-shot Winchester in his saddle scabbard.

There was trouble down there, all right. He could feel it in his bones. But he had a job to do. And he would do it.

He tugged his low pinch-crowned hat down over the long kinky hair that twisted over his ears, flicked the rawhide thong off the hammer of his six-shooter, nudged the buckskin off the rim at a slant, heading down toward the town.

Holding his horse to a slow clip-clop down the north-south street, he roamed his eyes over the town he hadn't seen in a good while, his ears taking in the sounds.

7

The town was fairly new, had sprung up along the path of the vast longhorn herds after the late War Between the States had cut adrift men no longer needed and made wild longhorn cows profitable at eastern beef markets.

Down the street the tinkle of tinny music from a player piano wafted out from a false-fronted saloon. A hardware and feed store and a buffalo-hide yard were on the right. A man carrying a pitchfork and a bushel basket crossed the street. Two hide hunters were sorting and stacking flint hides. A woman pulling along a child came out of the dry-goods store on the left.

At the end of the main street he swung his horse toward the livery stable he was looking for.

A merchant in front of the hardware store turned in his steps, watching the rider's back. Two loafers on a bench in front of Dewey's Saloon exchanged glances, not liking the black rider parading down the street as if he owned the town.

The black man had swung down from the buckskin at the water trough and was taking steps toward the livery door when a big, stoop-shouldered man stepped into the door space. A leather apron hung down to the top of his miner's boots, his flannel long johns visible behind an open-necked shirt. Obviously a blacksmith.

At the sight of the tawny-complexioned black man, the smithy's thought of making money vanished. "Something I can do for you?" His voice was flat, unfriendly.

"Train from Franklin come in this morning brought horses for Mr. Driskill. I got orders to pick 'em up. Name's Cole Granger."

The blacksmith had a huge head, close-cropped hair, and heavy, solid jaws. His eyebrows were two curved bristle brushes singed colorless from working over many hot fires. Muscles in his forearms strained the fabric of his rolled-up sleeves.

"Train come in, all right," he said curtly. "Horses out

back yonder.'' He jerked a thumb in that direction. ''But I ain't turning them over to you,'' he said smartly, dismissively.

Cole had expected as much. But he had a job to do.

Patiently he shucked a work glove, reached behind his shellbelt, and retrieved the note Driskill had written. Driskill knew how the town was.

''This'll explain things,'' he said, then paused, letting the livery man read the note. ''I'm Cole Granger like the note says. Work a small spread next to MFD range and hire on time to time. Be glad to put my name to paper for them horses if that'll satisfy you.''

The smithy was a big man, but Cole was no small fry. In fact, Cole was an inch over six feet tall and weighed one eighty.

The blacksmith looked up from the note, eyeing Cole coolly. ''I ain't the one you got to satisfy. Harvey Snowden, the agent down to the train station, he's paying the feed bill and board for the horses. You want 'em, you see him.'' There was finality in the big man's voice. He turned away and walked off.

The black men who pushed out on the western frontier were men of all calibers: men who had fought in the Civil War, got discharged, and stayed put; men from the East in search of better prospects; and former slaves who had used their new freedom to go West in search of a decent living.

During the years of Reconstruction some five thousand former slaves worked as cowpunchers, horse wranglers, bull-whackers, and teamsters. Some took up land as homesteaders. The more prosperous latecomers bought land. Still others, such as Nat Love, took to the outlaw trail.

Love was a short, wiry, dark-skinned man of no more than a hundred and forty pounds. He was known widely as a top hand by all the big ranchmen, and was a welcomed hire during roundup time . . . until Nat went into business for himself. His rope grew too long and reckless.

Nat had figured he could make more money running long-horn cows across the river into Mexico than by branding them for twenty dollars a month for somebody else. He was the first man the posse hanged, then his white trail partners were accorded the same rites.

But in general, the black man was still a mystery to most whites. Some saw him as a thing to be distrusted; others felt he was to be shunned. A rare few felt he was a good loyal worker; most felt he was lazy and shiftless. And former rebels blamed him for the Civil War. Accused him of being indolent, without care. Such men treated the black man as less than a regular hand, a mere tool to work, never to be taken seriously. Respect was out of the question.

The train station was a crude shack fifty yards southeast of town. The agent was Harvey Snowden, as the smithy had told Cole.

Harvey was pint-sized, shifty-eyed, his face deep red, and he talked fast. He lifted his eyes from the note Cole had just handed him, roaming them up and down the height of the obviously mixed-blooded man standing before him. "This's Mr. Driskill's handwriting, all right, but I ain't sure about this. When Mr. Driskill got freight coming in, he generally comes in hisself, or sends one of his hands. Never seen you before."

Cole shifted his weight impatiently. "I work for him time to time. Two days ago Indians made off with more than twenty head of MFD riding stock. Every hand Mr. Driskill got is out chasing them."

The agent wagged his head from side to side, distressed over the difficult spot Cole had him in. "Them's mighty expensive horses. I'd hate to turn them over to the wrong man."

The implication was clear to Cole. But it was known that horse thieving and cattle rustling were rampant, a thing to be looked out for. And thieves could dream up some mighty ingenious ways when outright thievery was too chancy. Cole knew the agent was only being careful; it paid for a man to look before he leaped. "Can't say as I blame you, but you ain't turning them over to the wrong man," Cole said reassuringly.

The agent lifted his eyebrows skeptically. Cole continued: "Be glad to sign for the horses. I aim to have them with me when I leave." Cole's voice was telling, the implication clear.

Harvey knew Frank Driskill only by sight, but he had heard the man was a good judge of stock and men. "I ain't saying you ain't who you say you are. All I'm saying is that I ain't got no rightful permission to turn them animals over to you."

Cole had known brush-offs before. Mindless put-downs.

But he was having none of it now. "If I was a white man, that paper would do," Cole said, pointing at Driskill's note in Snowden's fingers. Cole's voice stiffened. "I ain't no white man, but it's gonna have to do."

Harvey studied the note again, squinting carefully at the signature, stalling for a thought. Finally he slumped his shoulders resignedly, took steps to the counter. "No use to get your dander up. Freight comes in here, it's my job to see it gets where it's supposed to go. Man can't be too careful." Harvey slid a manifest onto the counter. There was distress in Harvey's voice when he spoke. "I'm trustin' you to be who you say you are," he warned. "You make your mark on this here, showing you got possession of them horses."

Few men out here, white or black, could read or write. But Cole had been taught. Harvey looked on in surprise as Cole scratched out his signature.

Harvey handed Cole back a copy. "You show that to Mercer down at the livery. He'll turn them over to you."

Thirty minutes later, Mercer was standing at the corral gate looking after Cole sullenly, as Cole rode off leading two fine horses. Not that Mercer cared about the horses. What bothered him was Driskill trusting such work to a man fit only for stoop labor. A white hand from the MFD should have handled this job, Mercer figured. Driskill was plainly lording it over the town sending a black in here on this job.

The MFD was a fifty-thousand-acre cattle ranch pie-wedged between the north and south forks of the Llano River. The seventy-eight sections flared out westward toward the Pecos River. The MFD ran twenty thousand head of longhorn critters, and had been known to employ as many as a hundred and fifty cowhands during roundup. Manfred Frank Driskill, its owner, had come into the country some dozen years before the war, and after the war he had been ready when eastern merchants came begging for longhorn cattle as a beef supply for the East.

Frank Driskill had always been a lover of fine horses. He already owned two English stallions for his riding pleasure, but now he was branching out into horse ranching.

There was a great demand for horses everywhere. San Antonio to the southeast was the biggest horse market in the world. The army at Fort Concho had always been a ready market for good horses. Now more cavalry was being posted at Forts Clark and Stockton farther out on the frontier, and the Butterfield stage line had a route from San Antonio all the way to San Diego, California. These operations required a tremendous amount of horses, good horses. And that's what was driving Frank Driskill into the horse-ranching business.

The horses Cole had picked up for the MFD were big-chested Andalusian mares, claybank duns. Both had black manes, heavy tails, black striped legs, and a black streak down the back. Each was close to sixteen hands high. Driskill intended to upgrade his horse stock by putting the English studs to these two mares he had had shipped in from Kentucky. The army and the stage line demanded horses with more bottom than the wild ponies running free on the plains had.

When Cole trotted the horses down the main street, everybody along the boardwalk turned to admire them. The question was, how did he come by those horses? The two loafers in front of Dewey's Saloon looked at each other wonderingly, unwilling to believe what they were seeing. One was a tall, flat-chested fellow. The other was young, sallow-faced, no more than nineteen.

At the outskirts of town, Cole touched spurs to the buckskin, lifting his pace to a shambling trot.

Behind him the rangy, flat-chested loafer stood up lazily, turned in his steps, and, pushing through the batwings, walked inside Dewey's Saloon. The sallow-faced kid swaggered along behind him.

Dewey's Saloon was small, unpretentious. There was a bar down the left side, a half-dozen tables scattered over the floor. Skeet Wallace was in there, sitting at a table over in the corner.

Wallace was a gangling, narrow-shouldered man with deep-set wide eyes. A wide-brimmed, flat-crowned hat rested back carelessly on his head, exposing a shock of sunbleached hair. He was thirty-something, known as a reckless, chancy man, vicious at times. He had been a twenty-dollar-a-month cowpuncher on the Lazy J. He was called Skeet, short for mesquite, because he was good at brush popping—prying stubborn longhorn cows out of mesquite brush—which was profuse out on the Texas range.

Three weeks ago Skeet and his two saddle partners had been run off the Lazy J. They were suspected of hiding cattle for themselves while taking wages from another man.

The bartender, Dewey Sloan, was slumped over the bar, supporting his weight on his elbows, talking to Skeet, who sat at a table, idly fingering a deck of dog-eared cards. Dewey had already seen the black man ride out of town.

13

"They ain't to be trusted, I tell you," said Dewey. "Long as I had this place, ain't no nigger ever took a drink from this here bar, no sir."

"Any ever tried?" Skeet asked, amused.

"One did." Dewey smiled, amused at the memory. "Some of the boys from the Rocking T was in here. Believe you me, that darkie was glad to leave when they finished with him."

"Used to work next to 'em," Skeet conceded. "But I sure as hell didn't drink with 'em."

"You got to keep 'em in line," Dewey continued. "Now, you take that one what just rode out of here with them horses, he keep doin' chores like that, he ain't goin' to want to do stoop labor no more. First thing you know, he'll come to thinking he's as good as a white man."

Cole's thoroughbred horses suggested to the town that a black man had somehow outgained them, was getting ahead of them.

The two loafers weaved their way through the tables, pulled back chairs, and took seats across from Skeet.

The tall rangy one, John Ledbetter, shoved back his hat on his forehead. "Skeet," he said anxiously, "we wastin' time sittin' 'round here. We ought to clear out. With or without them beeves we got."

"That's right, Skeet," said the kid loafer, Joe Felder. "Somebody was to stumble into Clearwater Draw and find them beeves we got hid out, we'd be dead meat for sure hangin' 'round here. No use in pushin' our luck over a few tick-bellied cows."

Skeet eyed them both thoughtfully. He studied his hands in front of him. Talking pensively at his interlocked fingers, he answered, "Maybe you boys right. Twenty head ain't much, but they'll bring traveling money." Suddenly Skeet's mind hit onto something. His eyes came up, excited at the prospect.

Skeet glanced over at the bar, making sure Dewey was out of earshot, then, leaning forward on his elbows, said in a low voice, "That nigger what rode out of here had some mighty fine horseflesh. The right Mex'can would pay a lot of money for them. Trip across the border would be worth our while."

Ledbetter's lips curled into a twisted smile. "Skeet, anybody was to say you ain't a thinkin' man, I'd call 'em a liar myself. What we waitin' for?"

Ledbetter was thirty. He had been a saddle partner with Skeet for four years. They both were hard men, men who took what suited their fancy. Each had done his share of killing. Skeet was on the run from Santa Fe for knifing a miner to death.

"Let's go get him, then," Felder said gladly. "I'd take that nigger to Mexico if I thought anybody down there would pay anything for him." Felder was a young wet-nosed braggart. He wore his pistol butt forward and was arrogant to a fault. While working the Lazy J, he had admired the tough, heedless ways of the two older men, and so had attached himself to them.

Skeet Wallace, John Ledbetter, and Joe Felder pushed back from the table, got up, and filed toward the door.

"You boys leavin' so soon?" Dewey asked casually.

"Anybody come lookin' for us," Skeet said over his shoulder, "tell 'em we gone to see 'bout some horses." All three men grinned slyly. They came out onto the boardwalk, looked up the trail where Cole had headed.

Nothing.

But they knew the horses were theirs for the taking. No doubts about that. It was just a matter of overtaking that black rascal.

At the hitchrail they mounted up, and away they rode, tearing out of town at a fast gallop.

Dewey watched from the batwings as they rode out, leaving a ribbon of trail dust toward the southwest. He smiled knowingly, turned, and strolled back behind the bar.

The sun was directly overhead, flaming out from a blue sky fleeced here and there with white puffballs of clouds. It was hot. Heat waves shimmered in the distance, and buffalo grass curled up against the sun's punishing rays. It was a land where a man's sweat never dried. Some trickled down Cole's back, leaving a dark swath on his shirt.

It was rough, wild country. The Immigrant Road from San Antonio to El Paso was just establishing itself as the preferred route, also the route the stage took. It was a well-defined road, but dangerous. Horse thieves, murderers, and cutthroats preyed on tenderfoots and unsuspecting travelers. Roving bands of Mescalero Apaches were a constant danger.

Cole was a long ways from being a tenderfoot. Twice he had trailed cows to Dodge City, Kansas, once as a wrangler and once as a puncher, both times with the Littlefield Cattle Company from around the Medina River area. Plus he had freighted in and out of Fort Concho. Frank Driskill practically made him come back and try his hand at ranching. He knew the country, all right. And he knew men.

Under the skimpy shade of a mesquite tree, Cole pulled to a halt and twisted around in the saddle, ranging his eyes along his backtrail. A tint of brown hung on the far-off horizon. Cole reined the buckskin around, focused his eyes there. The stain of brown grew, spreading toward him, lengthening at a good rate.

Riders. No doubt about it. How many they were was open to question.

He dismounted, hastily disconnected the lead rope from the halter of one Andalusian, and tied the bitter end of the lead rope of the other horse to the halter, hitching the horses in tandem. No matter what happened, the two thoroughbreds would be held together.

Quickly unsheathing his Winchester, he tied his own horse to a low-hanging branch. He hoped he was wrong about those riders. But in his gut, he knew they meant trouble. He waited, hoping against hope.

The three riders stopped just where he had left the stage road. They found his tracks leading away from the trail.

The lead rider, Skeet Wallace, swung his horse onto Cole's trail, came on at a walk. Ledbetter and Felder split off on each side of him.

Cole worked the action of his Winchester, jacked a round into the chamber, waiting.

They got within a hundred yards, and Cole triggered off a warning shot, kicking up a trough of dirt in front of Skeet's horse. The horse flinched, sidestepped. Skeet regained control, jabbed spurs to his horse, whipping out his pistol.

"Let's get that bastard!" Skeet said, gritting his teeth.

Those were the last words anybody on this earth heard from Skeet.

Cole's Winchester belched and jumped again. Ninety-five grams of gunpowder exploded, throwing out thirty-six grams of lead that ripped a small hole going into Skeet's chest and dug a big hole coming out his back. Skeet was dead before his next heartbeat.

Ledbetter and Felder came on at a full-out run now. Felder fired. A bullet clipped branches over Cole's head, whined off into the trees.

Cole fired at the flash. A slug tore into Ledbetter's shoulder, slumping him over in the saddle. His horse veered off, but Ledbetter held on precariously.

Felder never got off a shot. He swung his horse in behind Ledbetter's, and they lumbered off heading west.

The frontier was littered with bleached bones of cow ponies, buffaloes, beeves, and men. The bones of immigrants nobody ever heard from again, buffalo hunters, isolated ranchers, and Indians were all rotting out there. The bones of Andrew "Skeet" Wallace would join the grim display. When Cole rode away from there, he left Skeet lying where he had fallen.

Cole swung west, keeping off the Immigrant Road, since it was likely to turn up other travelers, which he wanted to avoid. He took to hard, brittle land, unbelievably flat, slashed here and there with steep arroyos and feeder dry washes. It was a land populated by creosote bushes, blade-leafed yuccas, prickly pears, ocotillos, and scrub mesquite. Making their home among these were spiny-backed horned toads, lean, quick jackrabbits, and the deadly Texas rattler. Ciboleros, or Mexican buffalo hunters, and Mescalero Apaches traveled the land hunting for dwindling buffalo. And scalps. Water for anything and anybody was scarce.

The sun was a brassy disk half dipped below the horizon when the land turned to rolling prairie of gramma grass broken only with mottes of live oak and walnut trees. Cole swung the buckskin toward a copse of deep green, broad-leafed growth off in the distance. He had put at least twenty miles between himself and his earlier troubles.

At the rim of a shallow draw leading to the copse Cole drew up, scouting his eyes around. The bottom of the draw was bone dry, studded with well-turned rocks. The white limestone slopes were covered with prickly pears, some twenty feet across. Thirty feet down at the bottom of the draw, a clump of stunted willow trees sent their roots deep in search of water.

This was Buckhorn Draw. A mile farther south it ran into Devil's River. Devil's River didn't live up to its name; eleven months out of the year it was bone dry, a bleached-white bed of sand and rocks. But when the river dried up, large pocks of fossilized limestone depressions still held water for a goodly time.

Touching his heels to the buckskin, Cole slanted down off the rim, rattled out at the bottom, trailing down a slide of rocks and sand. At a slow walk, he crunched over the dry bed. A limestone basin was off to the side under an overhang of white cliffs, ringed by a crude oval of willow trees.

Cole dismounted, unsheathed his Winchester, squatted on his haunches, studying the place carefully. Water. A scarce water hole. Any living thing for miles around would come. Especially Apaches.

He led his horses in. The basin was no more than fifteen feet across, the water perhaps six inches deep. At the edge of the pool Cole read the story of who and what had been there: wild horses, at least two mountain lions, jackrabbits, a rattler, and a pack of wolves. And dim imprints of moccasins—at least half a dozen Apaches.

While the horses drank deep, Cole moved upwind, dropped down on his chest, drank his fill, then filled his canteen.

A water hole at sunset is a dangerous place to be. Territorial animals, large and small, will surely come during the night. Cole knew this. He led the buckskin and the two Andalusians downwind of the water, scouting for a night camp.

Along the side of the draw under a well-concealed overhang fronted by a meager patch of gramma grass, Cole stripped off his saddle gear and picketed the buckskin. Untethering the thoroughbreds, he picketed them separately close by the buckskin. Horses graze peacefully in familiar company.

The moon was suspended far off in the east and a scattering of stars were out when Cole touched a match to the pile of mesquite roots he had heaped up. Shortly Cole was sitting on his haunches, a scalding hot cup of coffee at hand, and munching jerked beef.

This was wild, dangerous country. Many a traveler out here had never been heard from again. Whatever happened to them was a thing to ponder: Some had been arrow-shot to a pincushion by Apaches; others had been ambushed by outlaws and cutthroats; and still others had died of thirst and starvation. It was a land to tread carefully in, and nobody had to tell you twice to keep a gun close to hand.

Cole dashed the leavings of his coffee into the dying embers and stood up. Carefully he toed sand over the smoldering remains. Gathering up his blankets, he moved twenty yards upwind, and under the reaching arms of a stunted oak tree, he spread his ground sheet.

The smell of a dead campfire travels far on the wind. Like water, it beckons night movers: the curious, scavengers, outlaws, Indians, and thieves. That was a fact, pure and simple. A man couldn't be too careful out here.

Using his saddle for a pillow, Cole rolled in his saddle blanket and dozed, his Winchester resting by his side.

The wind was a gentle breeze that wafted in, bringing a dampness over the place where he lay. The moon threw soft shadows over the land, a million stars winking down on him.

The moon had swung way over in the west and stars had started to fade into vagueness behind a silver blanket of coming daylight when low grunting sounds disturbed Cole's sleep. He turned over on his side, pulled his blankets closer around his shoulders. The faint sound of horses stirring cut through the fogginess of sleep. His eyes blinked open.

Cole's ears were finely tuned to night sounds of the desert trail. He had slept many nights under the stars. But these sounds were different.

Keeping his body perfectly still, he crept his hand out from under his blanket, found the action of his Winchester. His ears reached out, listening into the night.

Random footfalls of horses milling restlessly came to him. The buckskin snorted, agitated at something. Squinting his eyes down the draw, he saw moving rumps, barely visible in the early light.

Suddenly he bolted upright, listening.

Small hoofs thrashing wildly about. A blather of wild, hungry squeals. Wild hogs!

Cole threw off his blanket, jumped to his feet. Working the action on his Winchester, he jacked a round into the chamber and focused his eyes into the faint light, waiting for a target to show itself.

Cole knew that in a ravaging pack, wild hogs are vicious hunters of man and beast, known to eat a rattlesnake whole, and slash a horse to its knees.

The buckskin was a range horse, and knew the danger. He reared, clawing the air wildly, two iron hoofs searching for a target. Ripping the picket peg from the ground, the buckskin wheeled savagely on the leader, a big boar with razor-sharp twisted tusks gleaming in the morning light. In an instant wildness came back to the buckskin. He rose up on his hind legs, nostrils flared to the wind, then stabbed down savagely, a one-two jab of his hoofs. The boar darted away from the stabbing right hoof, but the left hoof landed, a solid blow to the center of the boar's back, smashing him to the ground.

The hog squealed in pain, tried to dodge away. But before he could, the right hoof sledgehammered against his jaw, sending him tumbling. Dead.

A she-hog darted in, raking savagely at the hind legs of the buckskin.

The buckskin kicked back violently, then bolted down the draw.

The attack was an unfamiliar encounter to the thoroughbreds. One had wheeled on its hind legs in fear and had torn out the picket peg. Now she screamed fearfully and took off after the buckskin. The other mare snorted in panicked fear, reared on hind legs, ripped the picket peg from the ground, and followed.

Into this snorting, screaming scramble of things, Cole's Winchester exploded. A she-hog squealed and went around in a tight, crazy circle as if poleaxed in the brain.

Cole leveled back his Winchester and was looking for another target when two she-hogs broke from the pack, charging at him, a blur coming out of the dimness.

He fired.

Another hog screamed, went down on all fours. Quick as lightning, Cole worked the lever and swung his Winchester to the other hog that was charging down on him.

From out of the thickets a thunderous roar shook the ground and rumbled away down the draw. A she-hog screamed a death squeal and crashed at Cole's feet, thrashing out its life blood even as it raked razor-sharp tusks at Cole's left foot. With a wild scream, Cole leaped sideways, swung his Winchester to yet another target, and fired. Another hog squealed in pain. Again the roar of the big gun shook the surroundings, and a hog howled.

Cole was jacking another round into the chamber when the attack broke just as suddenly as it had started. Four wild hogs scurried off, snarling.

Cole stood spread-legged, braced against the recoil of his Winchester, facing the reality that the prize mares were gone, and he was afoot. Powerless to do anything about it. With a sickening feeling he turned his eyes to where the heavy gunshots had come from.

The thickets rustled, then a man emerged. Cole swung his Winchester on the man, sizing him up.

The stout-built man paid Cole no attention. He walked right past him, his eyes inspecting the four hogs lying dead out in front of them.

He was a middle-aged man, at least forty-five, big, and black as night. A thick gray beard covered his face, two thick lips showing through a break in the hair. His gray homespun pants were jammed into the top of miner's boots; a red flannel shirt sun-bleached drab was covered by a faded blue-jean jacket. He trailed at his side a huge rifle, a Big Fifty, a fifteen-pound Sharps .50-caliber buffalo gun.

"Been trailin' that bunch of hogs since four o'clock this mornin'. Figgered I'd catch up to 'em at this here water hole." He turned, looking back at Cole. "Didn't expect to find nobody here. Never smelt yo' campfire." It was obvious the man was a buffalo hunter; he smelled like it, too.

"Had a campfire up yonder," Cole pointed. "Mesquite roots."

The hunter nodded knowingly.

Out on the frontier a lot of men were wanted by the law for one reason or another. So where a man came from and whatever name he went by was his own business. A man was whoever he said he was and was from anywhere he wished to be from, and nobody questioned it. The thing was, a man had to be mighty careful whom he trusted. And you invited a man to your campfire at your own risk.

The buffalo hunter ran his eyes over Cole, appraising him. There was a hint of suspicion in his voice when he spoke. "You off the usual trail to be headin' anywhere." The hunter left that line of thought hanging there, and continued in a friendly enough voice: "You ain't likely to catch them horses afoot. Camp's over the humpback yonder." He jerked a thumb in that direction. "There's coffee and grub if you of a mind to." The hunter's voice was indifferent, a take-it-or-leave-it proposition.

Cole had to take it.

There was nothing Cole could do. A man afoot in this country was simply dead meat. So he went. With his saddle gun in his left hand, his saddle slung over his right shoulder, he followed the buffalo hunter.

Shortly they worked a way out of the draw. Almost at the top the hunter turned back to Cole, who was coming up behind him. "Camp's just yonder. Shame to leave them hogs lay. Hides worth four bits. Meat's good, too, if a man knows how to draw off the musk.'' He didn't say any more, just headed east.

The hunter was a swift walker. Cole trailed along in his long steps. And with every step Cole took he vowed under his breath he'd recover Driskill's valuable horses. Cole had seen in too many white men's eyes the disregard directed at him and other black men. A black man was looked upon as unreliable, undependable. It was a thing that dug at Cole deep down, a thing that drove him.

Also Cole knew that Frank Driskill was a tough, no-nonsense man, a man who wouldn't sit still for the loss of two fine horses.

Chapter Two

The buffalo hunter Cole followed was of a breed of men who had come to Indian lands as soon as the army had made it safe enough to hunt buffalo in relative peace.

The relentless thrusts of Colonel Mackenzie's troops of the 4th Cavalry out of Fort Concho had swept Comanches and Kiowas off the Texas plains. Now only scattered raiding bands occasionally jumped the reservation to the north, ranging as far south as Chihuahua, Mexico, their ancient raiding territory.

The hunters killed buffalo for hides only. Millions of carcasses fattened buzzards and coyotes. The picked bones littering the plains attested to the wantonness.

The buffalo hunter—Spotted Jack he said his name was—led Cole another quarter mile or so across the prairie to his camp at Cheavers Draw.

"Here she sits," Jack said, turning in his steps at the rim of the draw. Taking stiff-legged jumps, he bounded down the sloping side of the draw, talking over his shoulder to

Cole. "Ain't much of an outfit, but she's paid for."

At the bottom of the draw an Apache woman looked up from doing chores, her face blank, her eyes expressionless. She looked Cole over as Cole looked over Jack's outfit: two Murphy wagons, four span of mules, a saddle horse, and camp equipment. A lean-to of buffalo hides stretched from one wagon to ground pegs. Both sturdy, wide-rimmed wagons were heaped high with flint hides, hides hard as flint rock and stiff as blackjack board. Crude meat frames stood off to the side, strung full with buffalo venison to be jerked later. The Indian woman obviously tended the camp while Jack hunted. The smell of coffee was strong on the air.

The Indian was staring queerly at Cole. "Found him over at Buckhorn Draw 'bout to git et by hogs," Jack said to her. "Never did git his name, but he's footloose. Hogs run off his stock."

"No horse," the Indian woman stated flatly.

"That's what footloose means, ain't it, woman?" Jack said tersely.

The woman rolled her eyes toward heaven, disgusted at Jack's teasing.

In no time at all Pocahontas—Jack said he called her Pocahontas in recognition of her homely looks and unflattering figure—had fried meat and beans in front of Spotted Jack and Cole. Around the campfire they sat, Jack talking.

Cole came to find out that Jack had been on the long scout with General Mackenzie when Mackenzie was sent out to kill or capture Comanches and Kiowas who would not come in to reservation life. Capturing more than four thousand men, women, and children, Mackenzie didn't have enough troops to guard the Indians and drive the captured stock back to the Fort Sill reservation. The Indians' horse herd, fourteen hundred ponies, was driven into Tule Canyon and destroyed, every animal shot to death. Mackenzie then force-marched the Indians back to the reservation. Spotted Jack resigned his commission as a scout over this outrage. That's why he was out here now, hunting buffalo.

With the plains finally cleared of Indians, eastern merchants streamed into Fort Griffin clamoring for buffalo hides to make into leather goods. Spotted Jack had been loafing around in the Flat, a rough, lawless community outside Fort Griffin, when the first eastern merchants came out. Jack had been on many scouts out on the plains, and had seen millions of buffalo. To Jack's way of thinking, and lots of other men's, making money from buffalo hides was like taking candy from a baby.

Now Jack was saying, "Collected my last scouting pay, bought this outfit, and me and my woman been in the hide business ever since."

Spotted Jack was a natural-born talker. And he was a known man as a buffalo hunter and knife fighter. But to Pocahantas he was simply a good man who could talk from sunup to last light. "Now, you take hoss ranching," Jack said. "Good money in that, too, if a man knows his hosses. Been thinking on trying my hand at it. That what you figured to do with them show-off horses you had?"

"Weren't my horses," Cole answered.

"Hosses like you had, a man could put together a worthwhile outfit in three, four years."

"That's the way Mr. Driskill figured it."

"This Mr. Driskill is got to figure again now that his seed stock is gone." Jack shook his head pitifully. "This's almighty chancy country. Man thinks he got something cinched, next thing you know it's gone."

"I'll get the horses back."

"Mighty wild country where them hosses will go. 'Paches all over. Man going out there better know what for."

"I know the country. I'll get the horses back," Cole stated definitely, talking around a mouth of fried meat.

Already squatting on his haunches, Spotted Jack rocked

forward on his toes, his eyes fixed on the crackling mesquite roots burning in front of them. "Funny thing about hosses," he said casually. "Hoss won't run alone. In a day or so, them two you had will be tolled into some wild herd. Unless 'Paches git 'em."

Cole stopped chewing, spoke through filled jaws. "I'm damned if I don't git 'em back, 'Paches or not. Mr. Driskill 'speck me to bring 'em back, that what I aim to do."

Jack could feel the conviction in Cole's voice. Conviction that was pleasing for him to hear. "This Mr. Driskill . . . he yo' boss?"

"I works for him time to time. But I got a small spread of my own to look after." Cole shifted his eyes, met Jack's directly. "It ain't much, but it's mine."

Jack's old eyes twinkled with pride at the spunk in the younger man. He nodded sagely, understanding the way Cole felt. "Man ought to set sail for hisself while he's young," he said thoughtfully. "Wouldn't care to drop your name, would you?"

"Granger . . . Cole Granger. Live west of the Llano, edge of MFD land."

Spotted Jack had been around, had been over the mountains before. He was a knowing man. "Cole Granger," Jack said resolutely, "I'd wager you'll get them hosses back." Jack shifted his squatting position, spoke pensively. "Funny how a man get drove to do something. You take me, now. When I pulled out on Mackenzie, he swore I'd never amount to nothing. Swore I'd never come by my own hide outfit like I said I was." Jack cut his eyes slyly over at Cole. " 'Course, you'd have to go over to Griffin to get yo'self mounted again."

"That crossed my mind. But I was thinking Fort Concho. Closer," Cole added.

"Reckon you do know the country," Jack said, grinning. "So happens me and my woman pulling that way." Jack smiled to himself, got up, and reached down for Cole's empty plate. "We ain't making no money sitting here jawing. Let's load up."

Fort Concho was located where the North Fork of the Concho River met the combined flow of the Middle and South Conchos. Directly in front of the fort a raw town had sprouted up, as they are apt to do where there are soldiers.

First a sutler named Bart DeWalt and his wife, Angela, moved in. Right after that a trading post, three saloons, and two dance parlors quickly sprang up. The town was called Santa Angela in recognition of DeWalt's Mexican wife.

In spite of its virtuous name Santa Angela grew into a wild, shaggy town. It was as far west on the Texas frontier as civilization had reached. Beyond Santa Angela was a wide sweep of endless untamed country.

Buffalo hunters, surveyors, and army patrols stopped over in Santa Angela for their respite. Trail herds pushing north passed east of the town, and cowpunchers came in to whoop it up for a last time before crossing the Red River.

On top of these, outlaws and whores turned up, eastern ne'er-do-wells, and hide buyers moved in. But honest ranchmen and ambitious merchants came in, too, with their families. Solid men like Dudley Snyder, Jerry Poinsette, Alex Howsley, and John Anderson. Santa Angela drew a population of all kinds and grades, and they mingled together, the good and the bad.

It was about two o'clock in the afternoon when Spotted Jack turned his hide wagon down Santa Angela's main street, Pocahontas guiding the other wagon behind him. Cole was sitting next to Jack.

"When we pulled out, weren't nothing here but DeWalt's place," Jack said, pointing. "And the hide yard." Jack swore softly. "Town ain't hardly fit to live in now."

Santa Angela had spread out some more. Three more false-fronted saloons were on the left side of the street, the first one, the Bon Ton, sending out a steady twang of tinny music. The hitchrail in front of the second one, the Waterhole, was lined with cavalry mounts. At the last one, the Fiesta, five horses stood slack-legged at the hitchrail, two with silver-studded saddles and the ten-inch tapidera stirrups preferred by Mexican vaqueros. Three of the horses had "Lazy J" burned into their hips.

The street was alive with activity. Both sides of the boardwalk bustled with townspeople. Two empty hide wagons jostled along in front of Jack's wagon, and a couple of spring wagons came rumbling down the other side. Four cowpunchers wheeled their mounts to the hitchrail in front of the Bon Ton and swung down hastily. A woman waved a handkerchief out the second-story window of the hotel, yelling across the street to a buffalo hunter who had just swayed out of the Bon Ton. Two other hunters came out the hardware store, lugging twenty-five-pound kegs of DuPont black powder.

The stench of the hide yard was strong on the wind. Jack headed that away.

The hide yard was a low-roofed log-and-sod affair. Off to the side was a heavy log gate that led to a huge storage shed covered over with thatch.

Jack and Cole dismounted and headed for the soddy, while the Indian woman waited on her wagon seat. Jack pushed through the heavy log door of the soddy, Cole following in his footsteps. It was dim, dank inside. Comanche buffalo robes for sale were hanging on the wall. Hunter's supplies overflowed the place. A foul odor hung in the air.

"Emmett! Emmett Rath!" Jack called out.

Rath came from behind a hide curtain screening a back room. He was medium-built, had on greasy buckskin trousers, was shirtless. Long baggy sleeves of greasy long johns flopped at his wrists.

Rath was the middleman between eastern backers and buffalo hunters. He was a shrewd buyer, took every advantage to line his own pockets.

"Well, if it ain't Spotted Jack!" Rath said heartily, a pinched-off smirk on his lips. "You almost missed out. I'm freighting out tomorrow. What you got?"

Jack knew hide buyers, Rath especially. Jack acted unconcerned, casual, fingering a painted buffalo robe hanging off to the side. "I'd tally, oh, a little better'n four hundred," he said offhandedly. "For a good price, I'd call it an even four hundred."

While Rath was thinking on this, Jack added, "Feller here in need of a good horse."

"More horses here'bouts than you can shake a stick at. Somebody's always selling. About them hides ... some mighty good ones come in here. And aplenty of 'em. Take a look out back!"

Rath drew back the curtain, a satisfied smirk on his lips. While Jack was looking out, Rath said gleefully, proudly, "That there is one million one hundred and thirty-two hides! Outfit come in here ... Joe McCombs's outfit ... with thirty-two wagons loaded to the hilt. He had sixteen yokes of oxen hitched to two sixteen-wagon trains. Fellow by the name of Colson was ramrodding the whole shebang. Said he had hunted the Big Bend country all season. Said there was more buffalo up there than they had time to kill. They just give up and pulled out."

Jack drew back inside. "Never seen the likes. Range talk is, price on hides done gone up. That right?"

"Now, Jack, you know ..."

"How much you paying?"

"Seeing as how I'm already nigh overflowing, I don't rightly need 'em."

At Jack's askance look, Rath said hurriedly, "But I'll take 'em off your hands at a dollar and a half apiece."

"Let's go, Cole," Jack said, turning away. "Rath here thinks I just come on the hunt yesterday."

Rath lifted protesting hands. "Now . . . now! You just hold your horses. Let's dicker."

"Them hides you bought from Colson, I want the same price you paid him. I already had words with one of his skinners. I know what they fetched."

Rath smiled thinly, said slyly, "You got me there, Jack. Same price I paid Colson, you got it!" Rath stuck out a hairy-backed, greasy hand.

Jack took the hand, shook it, unsure of himself.

Rath brought out his tally book, showed it to Jack. How many hides he had bought, the going price, and from whom, was written down, as his eastern backers required. The record showed Colson had been paid a dollar seventy-five a hide. The thing was, Colson was a friend, and more important, Colson was a white man. Rath would quote certain white hunters one price, write the draft for a higher price, then split the difference.

Rath wrote up a draft to Jack for the exact quoted amount.

At Twitty's bank Jack passed the draft through the cash window to the cashier, a neat little man with a sunshade over his eyes. He looked at it carefully, turning up suspicious eyes at Jack. Jack smiled wryly, saying facetiously to Cole, "I shoulda brought Rath down here with me to git my money."

The cashier looked at Jack humorlessly, turned, and headed for the big iron safe in back of the bank.

The cashier counted out the money, then looked up inquisitively. "You boys staying for the big celebration? It's talked up to be something special." He pointed to a poster on the side wall. "Ranchmen, the Southwest Cattlemen's Association, have one every year. Handbill there says they got a nig . . . says they got a feller who steer-wrestles with his teeth! Now, that'll be something to see.''

Cole and Jack went over to the poster. Cole read aloud: ''The dusky demon will perform the amazing feat of steer-wrestling a wild longhorn with his teeth.''

''Must be some kinda trick to it,'' Jack said dubiously. ''That ain't possible.''

''Be worth cash money to see him try,'' Cole commented.

Stuffing his money behind his waistband, Jack stepped out onto the boardwalk, Cole following. Cole commented, ''Livery's the most likely place to ask about riding stock.''

Cole turned in that direction. His eyes fell directly on a man standing spread-legged in the middle of the street, facing him. The man was smiling wickedly, an insolent, confident leer.

''You ain't got that long gun with you now,'' he said to Cole. ''And I'm going to cut you in half, then I'm goin' to feed one half to the hogs, and the other half I'm goin' to make that old buzzard there bury it.''

It was Joe Felder, the swaggering kid. Backing him up were four Lazy J riders standing off to the side.

Cole remembered the man on the left; he was the long-legged puncher he had seen crossing the street earlier.

Cole didn't know it, but the long-legged man was Jason Stepp.

Jason had seen Cole when he had crossed the street. He had rushed back to the Fiesta Saloon and with a taunting smirk on his face, had knowingly questioned Felder: ''That feller you said shot Skeet . . . was he a tall, light-skinned nigger with rawhide chaps on?''

''That's him,'' Felder answered indifferently.

''You want him?'' asked Jason, his voice goading, his twisted smile a dare.

''You damn straight I want him!'' answered Felder angrily.

"He's outside."

Felder stiffened. He stiff-armed himself up out of his chair. "Show me. I'm goin' to teach that black boy what for."

Now Felder had Cole where he wanted him. Jason and three other Lazy J riders stood behind him, two of them tough Mexican vaqueros wearing felt sombreros turned up at the brim. They both looked hard, dangerous.

Jack started to say something, but Cole waved him silent. "I'll handle this," Cole said, knocking the thong off his pistol, sidestepping out into the street.

Felder looked at Cole coolly, smiling bravely. "Before I kill you, I'm going to make you a cripple," Felder bragged, then looked back, grinning, to see if Jason had heard his tough talk. His eyes popped at what he saw.

What he saw was his four companions standing there disarmed, six black troopers standing in back of them.

The six cavalry mounts standing limp-legged in front of the Waterhole Saloon belonged to buffalo soldiers, black troopers of the 10th Cavalry posted at Fort Concho across the river. This patrol, led by Sergeant Travis Tate, had been sent here by Captain Nolan, their commanding officer, to escort the stage to Fort Davis. They had been waiting for departure time in the Waterhole, the only saloon available to them.

Pocahontas had gone quietly up to the batwings of the Waterhole and in broken English had told Sergeant Tate what was going on out in the street.

The tall Mexican had been the first to spot the troopers. "Senor, you make the big mistake," he said. At the sound of his voice, the other three turned around.

"No, my friend, you make the big mistake," Sergeant Tate answered, jerking a thumb at his men.

The Mexican cut his eyes over there. The grin vanished.

Five black troopers stood wide-legged in front of the

doors, their carbines trained out on the Mexican and his partners.

"Senor, you are mistaken," the Mexican said, flinging his
arms apart carelessly. "We are only observers."

"Out with the guns! And drop 'em!" Tate ordered.

The Mexican shrugged indifferently at his compadres.
They shucked their guns.

Now Felder was standing alone. In his own eyes he was
a big man, a comer. Now he had to prove it. Alone.

Felder turned back around, faced Cole, the smugness gone
now. Sweat broke out on his forehead, his Adam's apple
twitched slightly, his palms got sweaty. Right now Felder
wanted to be somewhere else.

"Took y'all for horse thieves," Cole said quietly. "Got
no reason to change my mind."

Felder tensed up. His eyes darted around, searching the
faces on the street to see who had heard. Horse thief. That
or nigger-lover was the lowest thing a white man could be
called. It was a matter of opinion which one was the lowest,
but either one was like a ringing slap to the face. Only a
coward would stand for it. And everybody along the street
had heard.

"Was I you, I'd ride clear out of the country," Cole suggested.

That pushed Felder over the edge. His face went white,
then red, and his fingers curled, reaching for his gun.

Felder's gun cleared leather, came up, leveled, the hammer
cocking back. Cole's bullet broke into his chest, searching
for his heart.

Felder's pistol went off. The bullet dug a hole in the
ground even as he went stumbling back, his finger straining
desperately to ear back the hammer again. Cole shot into his
body once more, the bullet tearing the last breath out of
Felder. He sagged to the ground, dead.

White people gathered around, staring at Cole sullenly,

talking in low voices. Somebody said, "He ought to be locked up!"

Another man said, "Or hung! Town ought not to stand for this!" Angry white people moved toward Cole.

The tall Mexican grinned at Sergeant Tate and said, "Senor, the trouble is all yours now."

Sergeant Tate called out, "Squad! Two paces forward! Hut!"

Five troopers stepped smartly away from the batwings up to the edge of the boardwalk in a firing line.

Sergeant Tate commanded, "Ready! Aim! . . ."

The white men froze dead in their tracks.

"The next man who moves is dead," Tate stated, looking seriously over the white men. "Spotted Jack," Tate called out. "Get that man inside! On the double!"

The bartender inside the Waterhole Saloon, where Jack hustled Cole, was a black man named Abe Dooley. Abe had been looking over the batwings when the shooting first started.

Abe was a thick, squat man, just a shade over five feet tall, about forty, bowlegged. His legs curved about as much as an Apache bow. He lived in a shanty on the outskirts of the fort, and had heard all the army's doubting questions about the black man's fighting ability. He was proud of the way Cole had handled himself, and the way Sergeant Tate had stepped in.

"Drinks on me, boys," Abe said, beaming, when Tate came in with his squad.

"All aboard!" the stage driver boomed out from across the street.

"We'll take you up on them drinks later, Abe," Tate said. "Let's go, men."

The soldiers filed out, mounted up, Cole and Jack at the batwings watching them wheel their mounts away from the hitchrail and canter over to the stagecoach.

Pride was bursting out all over Abe's face when Cole and Jack returned to the bar, tossed off the drinks Abe had shoved over. Abe said soberly, "Jack, you know this town. White folks ain't going to forget this." Abe cut his eyes to Cole. "If I was you, I'd hit the trail. And I wouldn't stop till I got where I was going."

"Cole here is shy a horse," Jack said. "Wild hogs got into his camp. Run off two show hosses and his saddle hoss. He's looking to buy or borry."

"After what happened out there, nobody'll sell you a boot to piss in, let alone a hoss!" Abe paused, considering the matter more fully. "You know something . . . a platoon come through here yesterday returning from a scout. Driving fifty, sixty Indian ponies tooken from Nachiti and his band."

Cole and Jack exchanged glances.

Abe continued, "Don't you see, Jack? Mackenzie ain't around no more. You ought to be able to wangle one of them ponies."

"Hell, if Mackenzie was here I'd still wangle one," Jack said, scoffing at the thought. "Consider yo'self mounted, Cole."

"Considered," Cole said.

"But first we got to see this here dusky demon throw a steer with his teeth."

Every white man who had been on the street of Santa Angela that day had seen Cole, Spotted Jack, Pocahontas, and the black squad of troopers disappear behind the batwings of the Waterhole Saloon. And every white man had gone his own way to spread the word of what had happened. Some said Joe Felder had been murdered; some said he had been gunned down from behind; some simply said nothing because nobody wanted to admit that Felder had been outgunned fair and square by a black man.

News of the killing reached Fort Concho. Colonel Grierson, the new commanding officer, was a tough, hard-hitting Civil War veteran. A top-notch administrator, he had been sent to Fort Concho to mop up the Indians after Colonel Mackenzie had all but devastated them. Colonel Grierson was also tasked to measure the fighting skills of black men as cavalry troopers, which the War Department figured were subpar.

Colonel Grierson didn't like his assignment, but he had it to do. When he got news of the gunfight in town, he was livid. Black troopers of his command getting into an altercation with white civilians was absolutely intolerable, inexcusable, sure to be a mark against his record.

Captain Nicholas Nolan was the commanding officer of Company A, 10th Cavalry. Sergeant Tate was one of his squad leaders.

Captain Nolan, a smooth-faced youngster on his first assignment out on the frontier, was standing tall in front of Colonel Grierson.

"Captain Nolan," the colonel said sternly, "your men were over there in town raising hob. The army's understanding with townspeople is to keep nigras away from civilians. What happened, Mr. Nolan?"

"Sir, my men were in the Waterhole like they were supposed to be."

Colonel Grierson leaned forward, rested his elbows on his desk, his eyes stabbing out at the captain, his voice a severe reprimand. "Captain Nolan, discipline has fled your ranks, sir. You get over to that town, get me a full report, and have it on my desk before the sun goes down."

Captain Nolan's face turned pale, then blue. "Yes, sir," he answered assertively. "Will that be all, sir?"

"That is all, Mr. Nolan."

Captain Nolan saluted smartly and spun on his heels. At

his back, Colonel Grierson's face slackened, his voice mellowed. "Err . . . Captain?"

Nolan stopped, faced around slowly. "Yes, sir?"

"While you're over there, go see this ranchmen's celebration." The colonel picked up a circular from his desk, looked at it again. "Says here they got a man who can throw a steer with his teeth." The colonel looked at the captain, disbelief in his eyes. "That's preposterous. It can't be done." Tossing the circular aside, he said, "While you're over there, find out what the trick to this is, Captain."

"It'll be in my report, sir," the captain said, spinning on his heels, marching out.

Chapter Three

The sun was still an orange sphere flaring out from the west when spectators started arriving at the north edge of town in turnout carriages, box wagons, ambulance wagons, and on horseback, turning off the eastbound stage road, pulling into the wagon park in front of the arena.

The arena itself was on flat ground on top of a knoll that had been cleared of scrub mesquite and briars, and had been ringed with a rail-and-rider fence. Stout-post oak corrals had been put up to pin the performing stock, with narrow chutes leading to the arena. On the north side of the arena, four tiers of crude benches had been constructed for spectators.

To folks back east the cowboy was brave, romantic, a ten-foot-tall adventurer able to conquer all even as he drove his longhorn cows across the picturesque plains.

But to the cowboy himself, he was simply a workingman doing a day's work around stubborn, dangerous critters. His work was bone-jarring, teeth-rattling. Riding, roping, and branding. And every cowhand considered himself the best at whatever it was he did.

Now cowboys came from all around to Santa Angela to show easterners and cowboys from other outfits just how good they were.

With Cole and Pocahontas riding the wagon seat next to him, Spotted Jack circled to the west side of the arena, looking over the great number of people who had turned up. The bleachers were overflowing, at least a thousand people, Jack guessed.

Jack pulled to a halt in back of the corrals. They dismounted, looking around at all the people and wild stock.

Inside a crude corral, rank mustangs buckjumped and snorted, nipping viciously at one another's hocks. In the next corral, wild-eyed longhorn steers clashed horns, shoving against each other angrily. A dozen or so cowboys worked the rails, keeping order as best they could.

A clatter of hoofbeats from the east drew turned heads, as people looked inquisitively, anxiously.

It was Captain Nolan and Company B, all white troopers. They whirled in in a swirling cloud of their own dust, wheeled into the wagon park, and dismounted. They filed into the stands, took seats.

The announcer interrupted the chatter of spectators: "Ladies and gentlemen, to show you the everyday working skills of the cowboy, Ned Bender will rope and throw for branding a wild longhorn."

Two cowboys opened the corral gate and stampeded a big four-year-old longhorn down the chute into the arena. Promptly Ned jabbed spurs to his horse, galloped within twenty feet behind the steer, expertly lassoed the beast. Jumping off his horse on a dead run, Ned went hand-over-fist down his rope, threw the steer cleanly over on its side.

"That's all in a day's work for the working cowboy," the announcer said. The crowd clapped politely.

Two more cowboys roped and threw a brutish longhorn steer.

A new event was announced: "Ladies and gentlemen, cowboys catch and break to saddle wild mustangs. Ed Spacer will show you how this is done."

Ed choused a wild mustang into the center of the arena, then dabbed a loop over its neck. While one cowboy held a tight grip on the mustang's ear, another slung a blanket and saddle on him. Ed dismounted and strode to the center of the arena. Taking a grip on the saddle horn, Ed stuck a toe into the stirrup and swung aboard. The two cowboys released the wild horse and dusted out of there.

The mustang pitched, buckjumped, seesawed end-to-end, twisting and turning violently. But Ed rode the fight out of him, the horse running in wild, leaping jumps, tossing his head.

"That was a fair piece of riding," Jack commented to Cole.

"I'd say," Cole answered dryly.

To the delight of the fascinated easterners, two more mustangs had the wildness ridden out of them, one by Ray Childress and one by Aaron Spell.

These cowboys were top-notch hands from their outfits, their abilities proven over time. In fact, Ed Spacer had once bet a doubting cowboy that he could put a four-bit piece under each boot in the stirrups and, without dropping a coin, break a tough, outlaw horse that had been impossible to ride. Ed won the wager.

Now the announcer said, "Ladies and gentlemen, the next event will be performed by the Dusky Demon. If you saw Ned Bender rope and throw a full-grown wild steer with his bare hands, wait'll you see this next event. The Dusky Demon will attempt this feat using his teeth instead of his hands.''

The crowd murmured, shifted restlessly. A thousand necks craned around, all eyes looking at the chute. Jack and Cole drew up on tiptoes, stretching to see better over the top rail. Pocahontas squatted down, looking under the bottom rail.

Presently a mounted cowboy stampeded a big four-year-old steer into the arena. A pall of quiet descended over the stands like a caught breath. Women cupped handkerchiefs over their mouths. There was sure to be blood and gore on the ground. There simply was no way a man could battle such a brute. With his teeth, no less!

The steer had horns at least five feet across, gleaming in the dwindling sunlight. It weighed close to a thousand pounds, his brisket a tight bunch of muscles. There was a wild look to his eyes, and he tossed his head savagely, mad at his strange surroundings.

The cowboy beat his rope against his chaps, sent the steer charging across the arena, snorting.

Suddenly a big-chested bay horse charged into the arena, throwing back tufts of dirt. Bent low over the saddle horn was the Dusky Demon, Bill Pickett.

Bill was a little man, about five seven, weighed no more than one forty soaking wet. But he was powerful, his chest solid as granite, his arms two steel bands. He was thin-waisted, with short powerful legs. And tough as whalebone.

At today's big performance he had on a new black matador's outfit, deep-tanned cowhide boots, and a big high-crowned white hat.

Bill masterfully maneuvered his horse alongside the enraged steer. At the perfect moment, he kicked free of the stirrups and dived headfirst from the saddle, landing on the steer's back. His right hand deftly grasped the right horn; his left slid down to the left horn even as his boot heels dug into the ground. The Demon shoved down hard on the left horn,

43

at the same time pulling up on the right horn.

The steer's nose came up.

The Demon struck. Quick as a rattler, Bill plunged his teeth in, chomping down hard on the steer's lip, a powerful bite.

The steer stopped. Stood stock-still.

Standing spread-legged in the middle of the arena, the steer's lip in his powerful jaws, the Demon threw both arms apart, posing. Letting everybody see that only his pearly white teeth were being used.

After a long minute, the Demon calmly stepped back, flopped to the ground, bringing the steer to the ground along with him.

People were stunned. Awed silent. Suddenly wild applause burst out, whistles erupted. Thunderous ovations cascaded down.

"Well, I'll be damned!" said Spotted Jack.

"Never seen nothin' like it," Cole commented, amazed.

The Demon released his bite on the steer's lip and stood up. With a flourish of his other hand, he removed his white hat, doffed it grandly to the crowd.

Again a hush came over the people, the silence ominous.

The Demon's bronze face had soberly reminded the white people that a colored man had performed this amazing thing.

Captain Nolan's face flamed, crimson. He had detected no trick. The feat was real. "Sergeant, mount the men," he ordered weakly, still stunned.

"Ladies and gentlemen, that concludes our program," the announcer's voice boomed.

The stands slowly emptied, white people walking out silently, somberly, not knowing what to think, mulling over the implications of a colored man doing that.

Bill was walking across the empty arena, heading for the chute. At the east railing, his eyes caught sight of Cole and the others walking across the arena toward the wagon.

"Friend, that was something," Jack said.

"Been doing it free for years," said the Demon, smiling broadly. "Never figured I'd make twelve dollars a week at it, though."

"How'd you come by a thing like that?" Cole asked.

"Once seen a sheepdog at work. An old mossy-horned bull came in amongst the sheep and that dog chomped down on the bull's lip. Well, that old bull didn't move a muscle, just followed that dog along meekly just like one of them lambs. Right there is where I got my idea."

"Ain't that the damndest thing, Spotted Jack?"

"It's fact, though," the Demon said, and, looking over his shoulder warily, asked, "You Spotted Jack?"

Jack nodded.

"I was in the Waterhole earlier. Abe told me what happened."

"It was a fair fight," Cole said.

"Don't matter. Abe said to tell you he's heard talk."

"What kinda talk?" Spotted Jack asked.

The Demon looked suspiciously toward Pocahontas, who was standing off to the side, listening. Jack waved dismissively. "She's with us. My woman."

The Demon resumed talking in a low voice. "The town's organized a vigilante committee. They want to teach Cole here a lesson."

Jack smiled cleverly. "Cole ain't going to be nowhere 'round. Soon as I get a horse from the post, he's on his way."

"Abe said you ain't got time to go looking for no horse. He sent that bay yonder," Bill said, pointing in back of the corrals. "Abe said that's his own good horse, but Cole's worth it." Bill looked imploringly at Cole. "You got to git, boy, now."

"He's right, Cole," Jack said. "I heard about these vigilante committees. They ain't nothin' but a pack of white men

45

banded together like wolfs to kill. And nothin's ever done about it, neither. You got to git!''

While they were talking, somebody took down a span of corral poles, quietly hazed the stock through the opening, then shook a saddle blanket. The startled cows bolted, stampeding through the opening, down the chute, spilling out into the arena. In nothing flat the arena was a ragged circle of wild longhorn cows stamping around aimlessly, searching for a way out.

Cole and the others were trapped in the center of the arena, surrounded by slashing, clanking horns, closing in.

Suddenly a six-shooter banged. A bullet zinged by, tearing a hole in Cole's shirtsleeve, searing skin, whizzing on into dusk darkness.

"Let's get out of here!" Jack screamed, grabbing Pocahantas's arm.

"Follow me!" the Demon yelled above the bellowing steers.

Another bullet whined by Cole's head.

It was obvious the shooter was hidden in the corrals somewhere. But approaching darkness was throwing off his aim.

Cole, Jack, and Pocahantas followed the Dusky Demon, running in a crouch, zigzagging. Near the fence, the Demon stopped. Crazed steers blocked the way out. The Demon grabbed hold of a steer's horns, twisted his nose around, plunged his teeth into the steer's lip. The steer stood perfectly still. Other steers naturally went around them. With his other hand, the Demon motioned Cole, Jack, and Pocahantas around the other side of the helpless steer. Then, backstepping slowly, the Demon led them through the milling steers to the rail. Through the rails they went, Pocahantas crawling under the bottom rung. The Demon released his bite and ducked through the rails himself.

Another bullet smashed the top rail, whittling splinters into Jack's face.

Searching around in the confusion, Cole found the wagon parked off to the side. "Wait here!" he told them.

Running low along the rails, Cole dived into the wagon, came up under the seat. Crouching behind the seat, he undid the reins and shook the team into motion, heading to where the sound of gunfire had come from.

A silhouette moved in the shadows, a spur jingled. Keen eyes probed the darkness, looking for a target. A gun muzzle flashed. A bullet thudded into the side of the wagon. But the wagon kept coming.

The keen eyes widened. The wagon kept coming. The man backpedaled frantically, afraid of being pinned against the rail.

The wagon came on.

Fear gripped the man now. He fired wildly. Two quick shots slammed into the side of the wagon, one boring a hole right next to Cole's right leg. But the wagon kept coming.

The man panicked. He ducked under the railing, plunged through the horse herd, scattering horses, careening off flanks and rumps, heading for the other side of the corral.

Cole raised his head, looking over the sideboards, his pistol ready. The man he saw was no more than a blur, dodging through stamping, snorting horses.

Cole hauled back on the lines, brought the team to a rolling stop. Vaulting out of the wagon, he took off after the man, running low, swerving.

Advancing carefully, shielded by milling horses, Cole worked his way forward, eyes alert, watching for any sudden movement. Suddenly hoofbeats clattered in the darkness, going away from him. Immediately a big gun boomed, shaking the arena like a thunderclap, rumbling off.

Cole holstered his gun, worked his way back through the horse herd, emerged from the shadows of the corral.

"Cole!" Spotted Jack called out, rushing up, gasping for breath. "Seen two men. They took out. One's dead out yonder.'' Spotted Jack had the big buffalo gun in his hand, Pocahontas right behind him. '' 'Course, he ain't fit to tell us nothing about the one that got away,'' Jack commented dryly.

On their way to look at the dead man, Cole asked, ''Where's Bill?''

''Bill said the only way his handler would bring him to this town was if the Association promised to put him up for safekeeping inside the fort after the show. That's where he went.''

''Figured white men wouldn't like being bested, that it?'' Cole asked.

''That's gospel truth,'' Jack replied. Standing over the dead man, Jack continued, ''This one won't object no more.''

Cole toed the dead man over, turning his face up to the moonlight. It was Jason Stepp, the long-legged cowboy who had been in the street with the two Mexicans backing up Joe Felder. Jack's .45 slug had struck Jason in the center of the back, cutting his spinal cord in two. His mouth was still open where he had worked at words before his blood had drained out on the ground.

A quarter-moon hung in the sky; scattered stars twinkled down on Santa Angela. The buffalo hunter's empty wagon came clattering down the main street. Spotted Jack and Pocahontas rode the wagon seat, a tall, tawny-complected man riding a bay horse alongside.

A foul odor from behind Dewalt's hide yard wafted on the wind. Down the street a dog yapped incessantly. A woman's throaty voice reached out from the Silver Dollar into the night. The sound of cheap, tinkly music drifted out from the Bon Ton.

Cole swung the bay to the hitchrail in front of the Waterhole; Jack took the wagon around into the alley.

Cole swung down, shouldered sideways through the batwings, looking around the room.

The place was empty. The fetid smell of stale beer mixed with sawdust lingered on the air. A kerosene lamp in back of the bar threw out the only light, making weird shadows on the floor.

The legs of a chair grated across the floor.

Cole whirled, his gun jumped into his hand, pointing at the dark corner where the sound had come from.

"Goddammit, man!" Abe blurted out. "What you doing back here?" Abe came out of the corner shadows of the bar, shotgun held in his two hands. "You like to got yo'self blowed to hell!"

"Run into trouble," Cole said. "That cowboy what was out in the street with them two Mexicans . . . he's stretched out up yonder at the fairgrounds. Another one got away. Rode in here no more than ten minutes ago. You see him?"

"I ain't showed my head since the celebration started. Vigilance committee come in here looking for you. Seven of 'em."

"Six of 'em now. The one who rode in here, where's he likely to be?"

"Cole, every white man in this town is itching to claim your scalp. You already killed two of them. They ain't likely to let you git off with it."

Cole leaned on the bar, mulling things over. "Maybe you right, Abe. I ain't looking for trouble."

"Best thing for you to do is hightail it out of here." Abe went around to the other side of the bar, sliding the shotgun on the bartop. "Something else you ought to know. Two Mexicans was out to the fort trying to sell horses." Abe paused, letting his words sink in, then continued. "Corporal Jakes knows animals. Said them was Andalusians the Mexicans had."

"How long ago?" asked Cole, drawing up attentively.

"Right about sundown."

"Sounds like Mr. Driskill's horses. I don't know how them Mexicans come by 'em, but I aim to get 'em back."

"They more than likely headed south with them. Army won't buy stock unless the brand can be proved."

"About your horse . . . in the morn—"

"You in there!" somebody yelled harshly. "Come out with your hands up!"

"Too late, Cole," whispered Abe, his right hand sliding over to his shotgun. "They back."

"Douse that light!" Cole whispered. His eyes searched the room for cover, his six-shooter clearing leather.

Abe blew out the lamp. Pitch black. Cole was behind the corner of the bar, Abe resting his two elbows on the bar, shotgun craned forward. Deathly silent. A moth thrashed inside the darkened lamp globe.

A shaft of moonlight streamed in, played on the bartop first, then crept across the floor. Fresh air rushed in. The back door eased open a fraction more. Soundlessly Cole shifted his position, eyes flitting from the front door to the back.

The back door opened slowly another foot. A soft voice called out in broken English, "Cole . . . me come for you . . . Jack waits." Pocahontas!

"Cole, git out of here!" ordered Abe. "I'll cover you."

Cole tiptoed to the back door. Halfway out, he said over his shoulder, "Thanks, Abe. I owe you one."

"Git!" Abe said softly.

Out back it was pitch black. Cole had to follow Pocahontas. At the alleyway Pocahontas said, "Your horse there. Go."

"Jack . . . where's Jack?"

"There." Pocahontas indicated a crouched shadow at the corner of the saloon, watching the men in the street.

Cole started toward Jack, but Pocahontas stopped him,

holding him back by the arm. "There is no time. You must go."

"Tell Jack some Mexicans're driving my horses south. That's where I'm goin'."

Cole mounted up, rode off.

Halfway down the alley the soft coo of a night owl wafted to him. The coo was slight, unheard by most but heard by those who listen to the night.

Cole twisted back in the saddle, smiled. Turning back around, he touched spurs to the bay, lifting him into a canter.

The coo was also heard by ears of an old buffalo hunter, a ranging man of the wide country. And Spotted Jack knew it was the signal to go. He backstepped away from the corner and, on legs of a hunter, trotted back to the waiting wagon.

Pocahontas gently shook the lines and walked the horses into the night.

A pinched-off moon hung over Santa Angela. Six men waited out in the street across from the saloon to shoot Cole dead. But thanks to an old buffalo hunter and an Indian woman, he rode away, heading south to find two big-chested Andalusian horses.

Chapter Four

A thick-chested, solidly built man walked out on the porch of the ranch house, adjusting the swag of the Colt .45 Peacemaker belted around his waist. He had on store-bought gray pants and a brown tweed coat over a blue checked shirt. A high-crowned Stetson hat was pulled down tight over a head of solid gray hair.

Frank Driskill ran his eyes over the half-dozen well-armed men sitting their saddles, waiting for him.

"Where's Mike?" Frank asked Jim Seely, his foreman.

"He rode on ahead. Swinging by Cole's. No use in all us going by there."

Frank was mildly agitated, his son not being here. "Why didn't you send one of the boys?"

"He wanted to go. And you know Mike."

Frank eyed Jim coolly, came down off the porch to his horse, took the reins to the blue roan passed to him by a tough-looking vaquero. Climbing into the saddle, Frank swung his horse around, facing his men. "There'll be no

52

shooting 'less I do it.'' Frank ran his eyes over each man, making sure everybody understood.

They did. Frank led them out at a fast gallop.

Manfred Frank Driskill was fifty years old. Battle-toughened. He had fought Comanches, drafts, outlaws, and Mexican bandits. He had hewed his vast empire, the MFD cattle ranch, out of wilderness through sheer will, guts, and determination.

In 1853 an emigrant party of South Carolinians had headed west to Texas. The wagon train was made up of twenty-six people: Frank's older brother, Dave; Dave's wife and five kids; Frank's younger brother, George; and Frank, with his wife and three-year old son, Mike. The eleven white people brought fifteen slaves with them, four belonging to Frank: Absolon and his wife, Janie; their five-year-old son, Cole; and two single male slaves, Tom and Will.

The Driskills had come to Texas in search of land to grow cotton. But the word they got in Austin was, a man could do well cattle ranching. The government was offering a square league, four thousand acres, to any family willing to settle. And wild unbranded longhorn cows were prolific in mesquite-infested dry washes and hollows, free to any man tough enough to take them.

Frank Driskill was. He brought his young family and slaves farther west. At the south fork of the Llano River Frank threw up a semidugout and started in the cattle business. For five years from that dugout Frank and his slaves fought off natural and man-made disasters, gathering longhorns, acquiring more land.

In 1858 Frank sold a boatload of cows, bought sawed lumber from Louisiana, and built a ranch house and bunkhouse. And he built every year since then: hay barn, livery, tannery, everything a working cow ranch needed. Manfred Frank Driskill grew to be the biggest cowman around.

In 1865 the Civil War freed his slaves, including a strapping eighteen-year-old named Cole, in whom Frank had invested time and affection, raising him like his own, right along with Mike.

Now Cole was overdue. Frank was worried—whether over the horses or over Cole nobody was prepared to say out loud.

Driskill was a hard-driving man. He could get more out of a horse than a Mexican vaquero or an Apache. Now he was riding at a wilting pace, a steady long lope. A half-dozen jumps behind him rode six MFD hands, their foreman, Jim Seely, in the lead.

Seely used to ranch a section over west with his wife and two young sons. In the spring of '59, Comanches struck. Jim's wife and sons were killed, his dugout burned, and four hundred head of cattle run off. Seely gave up ranching, came back to the settlement for protection. Six months later, Frank hired him on as foreman.

Seely was a good man, steady, reliable. He had stuck by Driskill's side in '65 when Driskill's slaves left, and Frank fought with his family and town gossip to keep Cole there, giving him land next to the MFD. The MFD was the same as home to Seely, and Frank was family.

Now Seely knew Frank was in a foul mood: Cole two days overdue, and two thoroughbred mares and seed stock gone. Frank was hopping mad.

The ranch was three miles back when a lone rider came in from the east, angled into the tight knot of riders, swung his horse in stride with Frank's. It was Mike.

Mike Driskill was six feet tall, just turned twenty-one, and was solidly built, thick-sided like his dad. And like his dad, he had a head of his own. Some said he was the spitting image of his father at that age, physically and temperamentally. But he was a top-notch hand, the best. And he was in line to take over the MFD someday.

"He ain't been there, Pa," Mike said, riding alongside his father. "Tracks old. His animals ain't pinned up."

"Figured that," Frank growled. "Wouldn't be like Cole to come in and ask for help."

"Where you reckon he's at?"

"That buffalo hunter sent word he's headed south. And by God that's likely where he's headed if that's where them Mexicans went. I wouldn't give a plugged nickel for their chances, either. I ain't worried about Cole in a stand-up fight. It's them vigilantes that worry me." Frank gigged his roan into a gallop.

A little past high noon, eight MFD riders came tearing down the main street of Santa Angela and swung to the hitch-rail in front of the sheriff's office, every horse in the bunch lathered heavy, breathing hard.

Three gun hands loafing on the bench outside the sheriff's door were watching the MFD men when they rode up and dismounted.

Frank started spitting out orders as soon as his boot heels hit the ground. "Jim, go over to the Waterhole. See if Abe can shed some light on anything. This man Spotted Jack said he was roughed up some." Turning to his son, Frank told him, "Get over to the telegraph office, wire Austin. Marshal Slade ought to know about Cole."

Driskill walked up onto the boardwalk.

One of the gunmen, a thick, heavyset, Roman-nosed fellow, jumped up, starting to say something.

"Keep seated, puppy!" Driskill growled, looking the man over scornfully.

The gunman stiffened, face flushed red.

"Just want to talk with your boss," Frank said at last. He walked on through the sheriff's door, leaving the hireling standing there, gaping.

Sheriff Ralph Tucker was a tall, lanky man with a thin mustache, just a pencil line above his lips. He was a puppet sheriff put in place to look after the interests of the people at Austin.

Driskill was halfway across the room when Tucker jumped up from his chair, surprised. Tucker steadied himself, smiled wanly, said, "Well, if it ain't Mr. Driskill. What can I do for you?"

"First off, you can listen. And listen good, 'cause I ain't going to say it again." Frank was standing spread-legged in front of the lawman's desk, his voice stern. "No use in me beating 'round the bush, Ralph. Somebody sicc'ed the vigilante committee on Cole. I take it it was Morgan Hamilton."

"You got no right coming in here—"

"Shut up and listen!" Frank roared. Leaning forward, resting both palms down on the sheriff's desk, Frank spoke coolly, ominously. "I ain't talking about rights. I'm talking about Cole! Now, you listen to me, and you listen good. You get word to Morgan . . . you tell him I said to lay off Cole. Anything . . . anything at all happens to Cole, he'll answer to me . . . and by Jesus, so will you!"

Ralph shoved his chair back with his foot. "Now, look here, Mr. Driskill—"

Frank snapped upright, and his left hand shot out and clawed a fistful of Ralph's shirtfront. A swift jerk brought Ralph partway across the desk, Frank sneering into his face. "You tell Morgan!"

"Okay . . . okay, Mr. Driskill . . . I'll tell him," Ralph stammered.

Frank shoved Ralph backward, the chair catching him as he went down.

"See you do!" Driskill said, turning on his heels, stalking out.

Driskill took long, willful strides across the main street, his Mexican spurs jingling, his pistol flapping against his leg.

Just then Mike stepped out of the telegraph office, came face-to-face with his father on the boardwalk.

"Nothing, Pa," Mike said, looking anxious.

Driskill swore under his breath. "Them Mexicans got

56

nothing but open country between here and the Rio Grande. Nothing to stop them from crossing them horses into Mexico. The country down there is run by Morgan Hamilton, and across the Rio Grande by Juan Cortinas, both two-bit stock thieves and murderers.''

Jim Seely walked up, his brow wrinkled. ''The boys're finishing up drinks. Thought I ought to get word to you right away.''

''How's Abe?'' Frank asked.

''All right. They just threw a scare into him. He says Sergeant Tate come in from a scout south of here and heard that colored civilians got to disarm. New law.''

''And?''

''And Cole's heading south.''

Frank swore bitterly. ''Morgan Hamilton's overstepping his bounds. Law like that ain't going to stick.''

''Rangers being sent in to make it stick, Frank.''

''There'll be killing for sure. We've got to warn Cole.''

''How?'' Seely asked.

Driskill didn't answer, just went inside the telegraph office. Mike and Seely followed.

Cole had cantered his horse away from Santa Angela, following the wagon road south. Scouting his eyes over the trail in front of him, he had been unable to pick up the new eastern-style wide-heeled hoofprints he had already noticed.

A mile south of Santa Angela he left the wagon road, angling south by west in a sparse, dry land of sand hills and switch mesquite, a land of coyotes, cactus, rattlesnakes, deep arroyos, shallow dry washes. It was a sparsely populated land traversed by border bandits taking loot into Mexico. Also a land where Apache raiding parties roamed.

Under a bright moon Cole rode a tight circle from west to east, casting for sign of the Mexicans' passing. He came across tracks of a dozen or so unshod Indian ponies, and once he came across tracks of perhaps thirty wild mustangs on the run.

The night air had gathered a tinge of chill, the polestar hanging low in the north, when at the edge of a narrow dry wash Cole reined in his horse, searching the pebbled ground in front of him.

Indian sign again.

Six or seven hours before, not more than a dozen Indians had ridden the high side of the dry wash, sure of themselves, making no effort to hide their passing.

Cole rode on warily.

Two hours later, by moonlight Cole had twice ridden wide swaths west to east, widening the circle each time, and still had not found the deep hoofprints the Andalusians were sure to leave.

Now Cole was beat, dragging from fatigue, his muscles aching from jostling. He swung his horse to the dark side of a narrow steep-sided arroyo, the moon's light only a dim glow. The walls of the arroyo were a shadowy slope of dwarf mesquite, clumps of prickly pear, the bottom an ancient streambed scattered with tumbled-down sandstone and gravel.

Cole rode on quietly. The bay picked a way through murky darkness, his ears coned forward for night sounds, his nostrils flared, reaching out for smell. A night hawk swooped low into the arroyo, looking for prey; somewhere off to the east a coyote howled and was answered.

Cole's eyes caught the black hulk of a huge tumbled-down sandstone slab. He walked his horse up to it, dismounted.

He stripped off his saddle and blanket, and with a couple of hands full of mesquite leaves rubbed the bay down, then leg-hobbled him. Pouring water from his canteen into a cupped palm, he let the bay drink only a bit.

The polestar was way over in the north, the night silent,

when he spread the ground tarp he carried in back of his saddle and curled up under his blankets, using his saddle for a pillow.

The morning was pale light, the air sodden with moisture, when a whicker from the bay disturbed Cole's sleep, his eyes snapping open. For a moment he lay perfectly still, listening in the dim light. Silence prevailed. The only sound was of the bay, tearing at mesquite beans.

Cole threw back his blankets, shook out his boots, and stamped them on. Belting on his six-shooter, he picked up his Winchester, scouting his eyes around the campsite. Nothing had been disturbed. The bay looked to be in fine shape, alert, ready for the trail.

The sun was just streaking over the horizon when Cole scrambled the bay out on the west side of the arroyo, heading south.

For an hour, by the sun, he rode the open prairie where nothing grew taller than a horse's belly. Any disturbed mesquite grass could be spotted a hundred yards off if a man knew what to look for, and Cole knew what to look for.

About an hour later, he found them. The heavy hoofprints of the Andalusians, clearly visible in the trampled mesquite grass. The wide-spaced tracks headed south, the Mexicans loping the horses, two, maybe three hours ahead.

Cole kicked the bay into a run, narrowing the distance.

The gentle prairie vanished behind him, turning into sandhills and switch mesquite. The bay's breathing came hard now, his sides heaving for air. Cole checked down to a canter, stood in the stirrups, ranging his eyes ahead over desert scrub dotted with mesquite, prickly pears, and broomweeds.

And he saw the Mexicans, far ahead.

The vaqueros were following a dim trail that led west to the Rio Grande. And judging by turned pebbles and rocks, the lay of bent mesquite grass, they were less than an hour ahead.

Cole walked the bay for thirty minutes, then swung west at a fast gallop. On high ground on a cactus-covered sandhill, he stopped, ranging his eyes ahead. The thread of a trail the Mexicans were following stretched on into the distance, losing itself in bright green willow trees. Water.

But no Mexicans. Nothing moved against the horizon. The desert had simply swallowed up the Mexicans.

Cole rode down off the sandhill, angling for the line of willows. A hundred yards or so from the tree line he veered off to the left, falling into the pebbled bed of a shallow dry wash, obviously a creek bed that fed the willows.

Warily Cole rode at a walk, his Winchester held across his saddle bows, his eyes seaching for movement. Suddenly a horse blew. Bridle leathers rattled as a horse shook its head.

Cole stopped his horse, his own ears perked, his eyes straining, searching.

Something moved.

Cole jumped out of the saddle, his Winchester ready. Focusing on where movement had come from, he made out a horse. Riderless. Ground hitched, standing slack-legged. Hugging the far side of the dry wash, he advanced carefully, rifle ready, finger on the trigger.

Suddenly he stopped, stiffening as though he had been hit in the face with a dipper of cold water.

The two Mexicans he had been trailing were swinging gently from the limb of a willow tree, hanged. Each man's head was choked forward grotesquely, eyes bulging out. Another range pony stood off to the side.

Where were the Andalusians?

Holding his Winchester braced in his hands, Cole came closer, surveying the surroundings.

Nothing.

The signs told Cole exactly what had happened: Six riders

had emerged from hiding behind a clump of prickly pears and had taken the Mexicans by surprise. Or possibly they had been men the Mexicans took as friendly, since the Mexicans had made no attempt to resist or escape. The Mexicans had been hanged for the horse thieves they were; or the riders themselves were horse thieves.

A hundred miles or so east of the Nueces River all the way to the Rio Grande, the country was sparsely settled. Wild mustangs claimed the land, running free on open range, there for the taking by men who cared to rope, break, and brand them. Good saddle-broke range ponies were a must to ranchmen. But loafers, men on the dodge, men of greed, preferred letting other men do the roping and breaking. Horse thieving was a common line of work for these men. Big ranchmen had had their fill of the depredations, and a bond was agreed to: Any man caught in possession of saddle stock unable to show brand proof was to be hanged on the spot.

A hanging death was a cruel death, the worst a man could suffer short of Apache torture. Cole had seen hangings while he was still a slave, remembered them painfully. He had also seen it as a free man: Twice Frank Driskill had hanged Mexican horse thieves on MFD range, and once Frank had hanged a hired hand because the man had started stealing MFD stock. Cole had also seen Apache torture while trailing with the Littlefield Cattle Company. They had come up on a burned-out wagon and a luckless family of four.

Hangings struck a raw nerve in Cole. The business of the Andalusians could wait. Stretching up from his saddle, he cut the two Mexicans down. He would see that they got home.

The sun was directly overhead when three horses splashed across the Nueces River, scrambled out on the west bank, and stopped. Cole sat his saddle, squinting into the distance, searching the horizon for the finger of smoke that he had seen from the sandhill. The other two riders stared blankly at the ground, both dead, slung across saddles, head and heels dangling, a felt sombrero swinging from each saddle horn.

The smoke was plainly visible now, coming from an adobe settlement on the shelf of a canyon. Cole knocked the thong off the hammer of his six-shooter, gigged the bay into a shambling trot, heading that way.

From the Nueces River to the Rio Grande was a strip of land long disputed by the United States and Mexico. It was dry, sparsely settled, lawless land inhabited by Mexican descendants of the first Spaniards who settled on land grants conveyed by the king of Spain. After the Mexican war the boundary was set at the Rio Grande, and most Mexicans simply pulled out, withdrawing west across the Rio Grande. But some Mexicans chose to stay on Texas soil. Such a man was Jose Louis Gutierrez.

Louis was headman of Rancho Los Ojuelos, a Mexican settlement in Canyon del Diablo where Cole now headed.

Water was scarce. But Los Ojuelos was an exception. Here dependable seep springwater trickled out of the canyon wall, supplying the only fresh water for miles around.

In 1857 Gutierrez built an adobe fortress around the spring. His hired vaqueros fought off Indians and settlers to make his claim to the land and water stick.

Rancho Los Ojuelos consisted of thirty vaquero and sheep-herding families inside adobe walls. Don Jose was now a big ranchman of cattle and sheep.

Cole swung the bay down the carrita, or cart road, leading under the portals, checked to a walk, searching the area.

In the center of the village an adobe square surrounded the freshwater spring. Half a dozen Mexican women washing there stopped, lifted up inquisitive eyes at the black stranger. A dozen children played off to the side.

Just inside the portals on the left a wide-brimmed straw sombrero shielded the face of a small man sleeping against the front braces of a jacal.

While Cole had his eyes on the sleeping man, brown fingers reached out quietly, took hold of the bay's bridle, bringing him to a walking stop. Cole looked down and saw tired, old eyes above a big shaggy mustache.

The mustache moved under thick lips. "Senor, what for you bring the dead?" The man who spoke wore drab baggy pants, a loose-fitting cotton shirt. A sheepherder.

"Figured they lived here," Cole answered, swinging down, walking back to the dead Mexicans, the sheepherder following hesitantly.

"Horse thieves," Cole said conversationally. "Both hanged back yonder cross the river." Cole lifted the first dead man's face and asked, "You know him?"

The sheepherder's eyes widened. "Mother of God!" he whispered, crossing himself. "It is Miguel! And this one, Louis." The Mexican said pleadingly to Cole, "Senor, you are the one who do this thing?"

"They stole my horses, but I'm not the one who hung 'em. The men who did this have my horses now."

A ragged knot of inquisitive women and children had quietly gathered. Three old men wearing straw sombreros gazed on sullenly.

Four vaqueros led by a tall, wide-chested man swaggered out the open-fronted cantina, laughing raucously. Suddenly they stopped, taking in the scene across the way. The wide-chested man in front had on a brown, broad-brimmed, felt sombrero, a rawhide chin strap under his lip. He wore a brown short-waisted brush jacket, bell-bottomed cowhide pants with silver conchos down the legs. He had a black silver-studded gunbelt, a bone-handled pistol in the right scabbard, a ten-inch skinning knife in the other. A short-handled riding crop was in his left hand.

"Domingo, what is it you speak of?" the wide-chested man asked in his own tongue.

"This man, Rudolpho," Domingo answered, indicating

63

Cole, "he brings Miguel and Louis . . . dead." There was sympathy in Domingo's voice. "This man, he says he is not the killer."

Rudolpho headed over, shouldering his way through the crowd. He drew up, facing Cole, his three henchmen at his side.

Rudolpho Antonio Sanchez was a tough, arrogant man, a strong-willed man of violence. For miles around Rudolpho and his outfit raided far and wide east of the Nueces River, stealing good saddle horses, selling them across the Rio Grande. Don Jose turned a blind eye to the raiding because gringo bandits engaged in like raids west of the river. The country was lawless. Always had been. That was how Don Jose had built up his own herd.

Now Rudolpho looked at Cole, eyes steady. "Two of my very best men." Rudolpho spoke coolly, concerned, sizing Cole up. "It is true, senor? You are not the one who do this?"

"It's true, amigo, I am not the one." Cole reached up, took hold of the gun belt around the dead man's waist, jerked sharply, tumbling the dead man from the saddle. Louis hit the ground, his eyes up to the sun. "They stole horses," Cole said. "Only reason I didn't kill 'em was somebody beat me to it."

"They stole your horses, yet you bring them here." Rudolpho smiled, a crooked smile that said he didn't believe Cole. "Why, senor?"

Cole left the question unanswered.

"Perhaps you think we are fools?"

"Knowed some fools in my time," Cole said casually. "But I figure even horse thieves deserves burying."

Rudolpho shrugged, spreading his hands wide. "Horse thieves? Senor, you have the thieves, where are the horses?"

Cole faced Rudolpho squarely, his gun hand relaxed, his voice calm. "Only proof I have is my word. The men who did the hanging took the horses."

Rudolpho's eyes flashed over to his compadre standing next to him, the short, heavyset one. Then they fixed Cole hard. "Senor, I think you are a liar. You are the killer, no?"

"No," Cole repeated flatly.

Everything was quiet. Tense. Somebody was going to die.

A child wailed. A flock of pigeons swooped down into the church belfry. People drew back uneasily.

"These men, which way they go?" Rudolpho asked.

Cole knew the Mexican was stalling, waiting for the right moment.

"That way," Cole said, merely nodding his head to the east, keeping his eyes fastened on Rudolpho.

Rudolpho's gun hand was poised, his left holding the quirt alongside his leg.

Cole knew the idle talk was over.

Each man stared at the other, neither man blinking, each man waiting for the other to make a play.

Chapter Five

"Rudolpho!" a stern voice called out.

Rudolpho stiffened. Don Jose.

"Where are your manners?" the Don asked pleasantly, chidingly. "Strangers are welcome here. Even one who brings the dead."

"You are with luck, my friend," Rudolpho said, smiling sinisterly at Cole.

"Luck is a good thing, amigo," Cole replied evenly, waving a hand at the dead men. "Without it life can be short."

Rudolpho's lips went white. He wanted desperately to kill Cole, but Don Jose had spoken.

Don Jose walked through the opening in the parted crowd, Dona Maria, his wife, at his side.

Don Jose was tall, a lanky man fifty years old. He was dressed immaculately in a black short-waisted jacket, a red satin sash around his waist. His black boots were polished to a high gloss; a black flat-crowned, wide-brimmed hat, silver conchos around the band, was tilted on his graying head.

Don Jose spoke reproachfully to Rudolpho. "It is unworthy of Rancho Los Ojuelos to be inhospitable." To his people gathered there, Don Jose said loudly, "Time does not wait for the idle. . . . To work, all of you!"

Don Jose stood, watching the crowd disperse. There was a tight draw to his lips when he turned back to Rudolpho. "The gringo horse thieves . . . they must be discouraged."

"*Sí*, Don Jose, we only wait for your instructions."

"These I will give. The cantina," Don Jose nodded his head in that direction, "I will join you there."

"*Sí*, Don Jose. As you wish." Rudolpho glared at Cole. Finally, with a sweep of his hand he ordered his compadres, "*Vamos*, amigos, to the cantina."

Don Jose turned to Cole, smiling weakly. "Senor, your words interest me. Perhaps you will join us in the cantina. We must talk of our mutual trouble. Horse thieves."

Cole agreed. To the cantina they went.

Guiding Dona Maria by the elbow, Don Jose ushered Cole through the door into the cantina with a flourish of his other hand.

The cantina was a crude affair, nothing more than a square room with a narrow bar along one side wall, four tables scattered haphazardly over a hard-packed dirt floor. A layer of dust covered each tabletop; a cat stretched out under a table in the far corner. Rudolpho and his compadres stood limplegged at the bar, drinking tequila.

The bartender, a thick, heavyset man, jerked up, startled at his honored guests. "Don Jose! Please come in!"

At the words of the bartender Rudolpho and his henchmen turned their attention to the door. At the sight of Cole with Don Jose, Rudolpho's back went stiff and his cold eyes flared.

The bartender ran across the dirt floor, pulled back chairs for his guests, hastily wiped dust from the tabletop with a rag. "Don Jose, your presence is my honor," he said, beaming broadly. "And you, senorita, such a pleasure it is to welcome you to my humble cantina."

The bartender's eyes rested next on Cole. He stayed silent, his eyes blank, his Adam's apple working. He looked back quickly at Rudolpho, standing at the bar. Rudolpho had bragged of killing Cole. Now the bartender was uneasy, expecting trouble.

Rudolpho glared at Cole, his gun hand held purposefully close to his pistol.

Dona Maria was prim, sitting erect, her two hands resting daintily in her lap. The bartender smiled sickly at Don Jose. "Senor, what is your pleasure?"

"Tequila. Only the best for our guest, Manuel. And you, Maria?"

"Louis, tequila does not agree at this hour. . . . Perhaps it is wise to wait."

"Nonsense," Louis replied. "Tequila, Manuel!"

Fifteen minutes later, Don Jose had told Cole of the repeated raids by the gringos on his horse herd, and Cole had related the loss of the two Andalusians. Dona Maria had scarcely looked at the black man during the entire conversation. Now they were on their second glass of tequila. Don Jose said, "The man behind our mutual troubles is Senor Hamilton. He is a powerful man with many hired men at his command. He wishes to take control of all the land west of the Nueces."

"A land war?" Cole asked.

"Si."

Cole lowered his eyes, studying the tequila in the bottom of his glass. "I see," he said finally. "Without adequate riding stock, land is useless."

"There you have it, amigo. This evening we ride to . . . shall we say, discuss the matter with Senor Hamilton. Perhaps you would join us. Your horses, they are undoubtedly there also."

"A fight over land is not what I'm after. But if the trail of those horses leads to Hamilton, that's where I'll go."

"The trail will lead there. It cannot be otherwise." Don Jose shoved back his chair, rose briskly. "Come, Maria, we must go." Maria got to her feet. They started to leave, but Don Jose stopped, turned back to Cole. "Senor, east of here is a settlement. Tubac. Senor Hamilton rules the town. Your horses will be there."

"You sure?"

"*Sí.* But it would be foolish for a man such as you to ride in alone."

"A man such as me?"

"Senor, I meant no disrespect. My vaqueros and I will ride soon. Should you care to join us, there is a mesquite grove outside of Tubac. We will be there."

Cole turned his tequila glass idly in his hand, thinking. "Tubac it is," he said evenly, lifting the glass to the air, tossing off the last of the tequila.

Rudolpho's unblinking stare met Cole's eyes. Just then Don Jose spoke. "Rudolpho, it is time."

"*Sí,* Don Jose."

Cole eyed the big Mexican and his compadres as they trailed out of the cantina in the wake of Don Jose and Dona Maria.

An hour later, Cole was atop a sandhill that was covered by prickly pear just this side of Tubac, resting under the thin shade of a spreading mesquite tree, his back propped against the trunk, his Winchester propped on the other side.

The copse of mesquite trees where he was to meet Don Jose and his party was at least a hundred yards farther up the trail. Cole's cautious nature had convinced him to wait here instead of like a sitting duck at Don Jose's chosen place. Don Jose had been friendly enough, but a man out here could never be too careful.

Cole had already gotten up twice and scouted his backtrail in the direction Don Jose and his riders would come.

Now he drew up to standing, and more from habit than anything else, picked up his Winchester again. Once more he shaded his eyes, looked on his backtrail.

Far back on the horizon a thin belt of brown hung in the air. Trail dust, standing out like a sore thumb against the stark blue sky. Mounted men, Don Jose's men.

It was hot. The hottest part of the day. The sun was a punishing thing, a relentless brassy disk stabbing out from the west. The air was still; heatwaves danced. A ways off a dust devil twisted off on its own erratic course; a swarm of gnats flitted annoyingly.

Cole pulled his wide-brimmed hat down tight on his head, adjusted the swag of his pistol. Stepping over to the bay, he shoved his Winchester into the saddle scabbard, swung onto the saddle, and set out at a canter, heading for the wagon road below to meet Don Jose and his vaqueros.

Don Jose and and his vaqueros rode out to Tubac within the hour. The Don and Dona Maria rode in the backseat of a Celerity wagon, the curtains raised, a heavyset vaquero handling the lines to a matched pair of steel-gray geldings. A half-dozen tough-looking, heavily armed vaqueros rode in a tight group covering both sides of the wagon, four riding in back. One man was riding point: Rudolpho Antonio Sanchez.

Rudolpho's sharp eyes caught faint movement from the direction of the swell. He stood in his stirrups, focused his eyes there. He saw Cole coming.

Rudolpho swung his horse, raced back to the wagon. He said in his own tongue, "Don Jose, the cur dog comes."

"Senor Cole?"

"Sí."

Don Jose ordered the wagon halted. Presently Cole rode up, glancing at Rudolpho, a noncommittal glance, all the while speaking to Don Jose. "You were right, amigo. The horses are there."

"As I told you, Senor Hamilton is a man of means."

Cole ran his eyes over the heavily armed outriders fanned out around the wagon. "What's your plan?"

Don Jose looked confidently, proudly at his men, all tough, seasoned fighters. He was smug, sure of himself. "Senor Hamilton is a stubborn man, but I am sure we can convince him of an accommodation."

"Horses my only concern," Cole replied.

"As you wish," Don Jose said, waving his driver into motion.

The cavalcade of fighting men moved out. The only sounds that could be heard were wheels cutting through sand, spurs jingling, saddle leather creaking.

Cole was riding in rank beside the wagon. Rudolpho was still riding out front. The convoy moved down the wagon road at a leisurely walk. A mile or so from Tubac the wagon dipped down into a ramadero, or brushy gulley. All hell broke loose.

Winchesters went off, a sudden burst of at least six shots. Four outriders dropped from the saddle like ducks in a shooting gallery, dead before the sounds died away.

Cole and the others jerked to a startled halt, riderless ponies pitching and bucking.

Like well-drilled brush fighters, seven men, all white, broke from cover, took up positions along the bank of the gulley, each man standing spread-legged, a Winchester leveled forward.

The attack had been so sudden, so thorough, that Don Jose's men and Cole were caught flat-footed. There simply was nothing anybody could do.

Cole's face was stolid, a mask of grim silence.

Backshooters and bushwhackers were a common lot out here, but this took the cake! Worst of all, Cole saw a badge shining on each bushwhacker's chest.

The ambushers fanned out around the party, Winchesters trained on Cole and the Mexicans. Another man escorted Rudolpho back to the bunch, a Winchester aimed at his back. Rudolpho said remorsefully, "Don Jose, I did not see—"

"There will be time enough," Don Jose interrupted.

Dona Maria sat rigidly, outraged. Don Jose looked deliberately at each of his dead outriders, then coolly turned his attention to the big gringo who was obviously the leader of the attackers. "What is the meaning of this?" Don Jose demanded.

The gringo was a tall man, a good three inches over six feet. He had on faded blue jeans, a brown canvas bush jacket, and a high-crowned gray hat. He was hawk-faced but had a solidness about him, and spoke with outward pride. "Name's Armstrong. McNelly's Rangers. Orders are to shoot on sight any man ridin' a saddle like them yonder." Armstrong pointed. "You boys are comin' to headquarters. Capt'n will want to look you over."

Don Jose was shocked. "That is impossible!" he said smugly. "I have urgent business!"

"Makes no difference what business you got. You'll see the capt'n first," Armstrong said definitely. "Jack, bring in the horses!" he yelled over his shoulder, walking toward Cole, looking him over. Armstrong said, with casual disregard in his voice, "You ain't a Mex, but the capt'n will see you too."

Armstrong ran his eyes over the men he had to escort. "I'm tellin' all of you right now, keep your hands clear of them guns. We got four dead men already. There'll sure as hell be more if anybody git antsy."

Neither Cole nor the Mexicans knew it, but Mexican outlaws had just the day before raided a settlement north of

Tubac. Three storekeepers had been shot dead; a stiff-necked, frothy white woman who resisted parting with her valuables had been quirted near death; the town was looted and sacked. Along with other loot taken, the gaudy-eyed Mexicans had made off with twelve Dick Heye saddles.

Dick Heye saddles were the finest riding saddles in the world. Besides being fashioned out of the best leather, the skirts were concho-studded with pure silver in large diamond patterns, and the twelve-inch tapaderas were also ringed with silver studs.

Ranger Captain McNelly, Sergeant Ted Armstrong, and eighteen other Rangers had been dispatched to the area to put an end to just this sort of wanton plundering. When McNelly heard firsthand of this outrage, his straightforward orders to his Rangers were, ''Empty every saddle on sight and leave the rider where he lay; bring the saddle and any accomplices in to headquarters.''

Now Cole, Don Jose, and his party were being led into Ranger headquarters. Four of the party's saddles were empty; the empty saddles were brand-new Dick Heye saddles.

Ranger headquarters was on the western outskirts of Tubac. It was nothing more than a horse camp with a Sibley tent. Captain McNelly had been alerted that the Rangers sent out this morning were coming in with a bunch of Mexicans. McNelly was standing at his tent flap waiting, a huge unlit cigar clenched in his stained yellow teeth.

Captain L. H. McNelly was a short, frail, consumptive man, weighing no more than a hundred and thirty pounds. Heavy brown whiskers covered his gaunt face; his dark eyes were hard, merciless.

McNelly was enigmatic, a man of shifting loyalties. During the War Between the States he had been an irregular Confederate soldier, a guerrilla fighter, operating behind the lines down in Louisiana. After the war he crossed over into Texas, inexplicably signed on as a captain of the state police organized by his former enemies, the Reconstruction Republicans. The state police turned out to be such a heavy-handed, corrupt bunch that even McNelly quit them.

Republicans were thrown out. Democratic governor Richard Coke took control of the state, and right off realized that hard, ruthless, but honest men were needed to rein in rampant lawlessness and blatant thievery. McNelly was the new governor's man.

"Come on some of them Dick Heye saddles, Capt'n," Armstrong reported. "And we emptied 'em like you said."

"Good work, Armstrong. Outlaws are going to learn we mean business." McNelly noticed the handsomely dressed Don Jose and Dona Maria. He said in a low voice to Armstrong, "Looks to me like you corraled some big shot Mexican and a bunch of fighting men. They got anything to do with them saddles?"

"They was all ridin' in the same bunch. The big shot's name is Jose Luis Gutierrez, the honcho over at Rancho Los Ojuelos. Them's his vaqueros. Says he's got business with Mr. Hamilton."

"He ain't a Mex," McNelly said, indicating Cole. "What's his connection?"

"Never asked. Just brought him in with the rest."

McNelly turned on his heels, ordering over his shoulder, "Bring the big fish and the other one inside."

Before McNelly quit the state police he had compiled an outlaw list, the name of every man below Big Bend country known to operate outside the law.

Governor Coke resurrected the outlaw list. McNelly had it, and had been ordered to prune down the list any way he saw fit.

McNelly was sitting behind a cracker box, his camp desk, when Don Jose and Cole were brought in.

"This business you got with Morgan Hamilton, I'm taking it to be gun business," McNelly said to the Don, his voice flat, firm. "There'll be no more takin' the law in your own hands. I'm ordering you to disband those men out there, send them home. Or I'll treat the lot of you as armed outlaws."

"But, Senor—"

"Morgan Hamilton will get the same word," McNelly promised. "And I'll see he follows my orders just as you will. Now, disband 'em!"

There were sixteen Rangers in the camp, all armed with pistols, and each man had just been issued a brand-new .50-caliber Sharps rifle. There simply was nothing Don Jose could do. "*Sí*, senor," he said weakly.

McNelly watched Don Jose leave the tent, walking proudly, his head held high. Turning his eyes to Cole, McNelly asked conversationally, "Your name?"

"Cole. Cole Granger."

"What's your business?"

"Trailing six men with stolen horses. Blooded stock."

"Frank Driskill's stock?"

Cole's brows lifted. "You know him?"

"Knowed him way before the war. Morgan Hamilton, too. These men, Frank figure they actin' for Morgan?"

"Mr. Driskill ain't heard yet. Leastwise not from me. But that don't matter. I aim to git the horses back. One way or another."

"That's what Frank Driskill would do, that it?" McNelly retorted flatly, his tone facetious.

"I was sent to fetch them horses, and that's what I intend to do," Cole said, rankled at the inference.

"Killin' and horse thievin' is Ranger business from now on. Not Frank's, not Morgan's, not your'n. Any man settlin' his own score with a pistol will answer to the law." McNelly shoved back from his desk, stood up, walked around the desk. "Consider your complaint duly registered with the proper authority. I'm ridin' into Tubac on Ranger business. Any blooded stock been run in there, Morgan Hamilton will know about it. I'll talk to him.'' McNelly's voice was pleasant. ''You ride on back to the MFD, let Mr. Driskill know about this.''

McNelly stopped, thought a minute, then said reassuringly, ''You tell Frank Captain Leander McNelly said he'll get his stock back.''

''Mr. Driskill sent me to fetch them horses.'' Cole looked directly, deliberately into McNelly's eyes. ''I aim to ride into Tubac. Unless you got a law that says I can't.''

McNelly was a pitiless man with a quick fuse. But he was sensible. His thin voice crackled, ''I don't make the law. Law comes from the statehouse, and what law comes down is what I enforce.''

''I take it you ain't got no law that says I can't?''

''I ain't got one that says you can't. But any man settlin' his own score with a gun is outside the law. That's over and done with. You ride into Tubac and stir up trouble, I'll treat you like any common outlaw. And I'll hunt you down like one.'' McNelly shifted his tone, became dismissive. ''I said my piece. You make up your own mind. I got business.'' He threw back the tent flap, stepped outside, and called out, ''Armstrong!''

''Yo, Capt'n!''

''Mount the men! Let's ride!''

Cole was walking toward his horse even as McNelly swung into the saddle and wheeled out at a fast clip, Armstrong and five other Rangers hard on his heels.

McNelly's ringing warning to Cole had spread quickly throughout the camp. The Rangers left behind looked questioningly at each other as Cole mounted up. They were wondering which way he would ride.

The Rangers knew Captain McNelly was rigid, uncompromising, not a man to push.

None of them knew Cole.

Cole swung his horse east, heading toward Tubac at a gentle lope.

Chapter Six

The town of Tubac had sprung up in a bend in the road where the Overland Stage dipped down into a shallow valley eight miles southwest of Santa Angela. It had begun as a dangerous frontier stage stop: Holdup men preyed on passengers; horse thieves rustled good stock; and Comanches took it as easy pickings astride their war trail into Mexico.

A tough, no-nonsense veteran fighter with an eye for a dollar and a hand for steady work took over the place as station tender. Hank McGowan, handy with pistol and Winchester, fought the station to safety and reliability, made peace with some of the Indians, and fought others to a standstill. Later his application to the government for a post office was approved, and the station took off as a coming town.

Now maybe a hundred people had moved in and around the one-street town: ranchmen, dryland farmers, merchants, a hostler and wheelwright, dance-hall girls, men on the dodge, they all were drawn to Tubac, with fair intentions or foul.

Morgan Hamilton had most of the town in his hip pocket. And what he didn't have already he had eyes on.

The sun was deep into the shank of the afternoon, long shadows stretching across the street, when Cole checked the bay to a walk down Tubac's main street, scouting his eyes around.

The boardwalks on both sides of the street had activity, and slack-legged cow ponies crowded the hitchrails, tails switching flies. Two boxwagons were being loaded in front of the hardware store, another one trundling down the street. Three cowboys loped their ponies from down the other end of town. A tall, thin man wearing a brown suit was locking up the bank.

Two cowhands loafing on a bench in front of the Golden Eagle Saloon eyed Cole coolly. One spit a stream of tobacco juice into the street.

Cole rode on, minding his own business.

The sound of a piano wafted out to the street, a woman's lighthearted laughter cutting through the sound.

Cole spotted Don Jose and Dona Maria in front of the Exchange Hotel, swung his horse that way, got there just as they mounted their rig. McNelly's big sorrel horse was tied up there, along with a half-dozen other horses.

"Amigo, where are your vaqueros?" Cole asked.

Jose smiled knowingly. "There is more than one way to skin the cat, senor. Morgan Hamilton will hear from me, you can be sure. And you, senor, what of your horses?" Don Jose asked soberly.

"I aim to get them back."

"They are here. Already men speak fondly of them."

Cole shifted his eyes to a queer sound. Clamorous jeering. Angry men. Coming from the alley.

"Trouble," Don Jose warned. "Unpleasant trouble I do not wish. *Adiós,* amigo." Don Jose's driver shook the lines, took out.

78

"Adiós," Cole said softly. He trotted the bay across the street to where the crowd was, next to the hotel. Checking up his horse at the edge of the crowd, he took in the scene.

Fifteen, twenty men, some black, most white, were grouped around a flatbed wagon listening to a black man talk. The black man was tall, thin-shouldered, wore a gray Prince Albert coat, white shirt, string tie. He had on a black stovepipe hat. He was silent now, lips tight, eyes glazed over, puzzled by the angry outburst his unexpected presence had drawn from the mixed crowd.

"Good citizens of Tubac," he said, trying to calm them. "You all know me. When I was your state senator I represented every man among you, white or black, fair and square."

"The hell you say!" yelled back a burly white man angrily. "Ain't nothing fair and square about a black Republican! Your time is over. Now you'll feel how it is to be trampled on!"

"Let's hear him out!" pleaded a short black man.

"Yeah, let Ruby talk!" said another black man.

George T. Ruby had been elected a state senator when Reconstruction Republicans, union men, carpetbaggers, and freedmen had had charge of the state. But they had now lost the election, so Senator Ruby and his party were out. White men who had suffered under their heavy-handed rule were out for revenge.

Ruby regained his poise. "All you men know I'm a fair man regardless of our political differences. I realize Democrats are in control. They make the law now." Ruby's voice caught as he continued, "But this new law that says the colored man got to disarm, every man among you know that ain't right!" Ruby wagged his head disgustedly. "To all my colored brothers, I say obey the law. To all my white friends, I say be fair-minded."

"You'll get the same what you gave us!" a white man yelled back.

"You singing a different tune now, Ruby!" another white man yelled. "The only thing you'll get from us is a rope!"

"There's more'n one rope!" a short black man roared back.

Ruby's face turned ashen. He raked his tongue over dry, heavy lips, his eyes darting over the unruly mob. "Now, brothers! . . . Now, friends!" Panic was rising in Ruby's voice. He lifted a hand for calm but it was an empty gesture. Ruby suddenly realized his coming here was a mistake. Now he wanted desperately to be somewhere else.

White men grew furious. The mere sight of Ruby had brought back bitter memories of years of Northern rule, first by a military governor and then by carpetbaggers and freedmen.

Somebody threw a solid clod of earth at Ruby's head, missing by inches only, the dirt smashed into the saloon wall behind him. Ruby's horse team pranced, jittery, straining at the lines nervously. "This's peaceful talk," somebody said calmingly. "No use'n gettin' riled!"

"I say disarm them now," the big burly white man yelled angrily. "We ain't got to wait for no law!"

"Yeah! Disarm now!" another white man agreed.

Another clod of earth zoomed by Ruby's head, missing by inches as he ducked away.

Cole had been sizing up the crowd, his eyes constantly roving over the men. He knew which ones were doing the agitating, who the troublemakers were.

There was a tall, medium-built white man standing in back, almost aloof from the crowd, his white flat-crowned hat conspicuous. Cole had judged him to be a man with a purpose, not a farmer or cowpuncher as these other men obviously were.

The white hat kept moving around closer. The man's gun

hand peeled back the tail end of his homespun gray suitcoat, inched up ever so slowly toward his pistol.

Cole knew the target was Ruby.

A shot fired now would set off a shooting spree, men firing into each other at point-blank range.

Cole nudge his horse forward, quietly walked him up behind the white hat.

Slowly the man's pistol cleared leather, started to come up. And like a brickbat from heaven Cole's pistol barrel exploded against his skull. He dropped like a sack of grain. But the blow was an instant too late. The man's pistol went off, spitting a shaft of flame, a bullet digging a hole in the ground, whining off harmlessly down the alley.

Every man in the crowd froze, every lip still.

Cole raised his pistol muzzle in the air, his eyes keeping watch over the men, alert for a wrong move. Directly he yelled at the man standing in the wagon, "Mister, if I was you, I'd get out of here!"

Ruby threw himself over the driver's seat. Standing up in the wagon bed, he whipped the horses into a run down the alley.

Cole ran his eyes over the angry mob, split along color lines now. Seven black men, nine white, all armed, plus one man unconscious on the ground. "Looks to be a fair enough fight," Cole announced, holstering his gun. Backing his horse out into the street, he swung toward the livery just as the man he had clubbed moved, shaking his head vigorously, throwing off the cobwebs from the ringing blow.

Finally the man got up, staggering in his steps, blinking back the throb. He glanced shamefacedly at the white men looking at him, then glowered out at the black men arrayed against them. "Who hit me?" he demanded.

"Stranger done it," the burly white man said.

"You was going to sneak-shoot Ruby!" the short black man said accusingly.

81

"Ira, I got no fuss with you," the white man said.

"You earned that crack over the noggin," Ira said. "Serves you right. Far as I'm concerned, it's over and done with."

"Yeah, it's done with," another white man agreed.

"Let's all go on about our business," somebody else said.

"That's sound advice for us all," a black man agreed.

The man who had been cracked over the head picked up his hat, quickly glanced up, looking at the second-story window of the Exchange Hotel.

Morgan Hamilton stood there looking down at the street, frowning, his two thumbs hooked in the pockets of his red satin-fronted vest, his jaws tight. Morgan was livid. His hired men had failed to kill Ruby.

Morgan was tall and spare, carried himself with arrogance born of walking over anybody and anything that stood in his way. His face was clean-shaven, his mustache trimmed meticulously. From under the brim of his white Stetson hat his eyes were dazzling blue.

Morgan had seen the black man who had saved Ruby's life. And Morgan didn't like it. He didn't like nobody getting in his way. He jerked the velvet window curtain closed, whirled on his heels, and stalked across the room, his high-glossed boots swishing softly through his deep-carpeted upstairs suite. "Damn fools missed," Morgan said to the man sitting one-hipped on the edge of the mahogany desk. He checked the time, lifting out of his vest pocket a gold watch on the end of a heavy gold chain across his vest. "Damn fools missed!"

"I told you that blockhead would foul up the job," the other man said, a satisfied smirk on his face. "What happened down there?"

"Stop your gloating, Ashbel," Morgan replied sharply. "You'll get your chance!" Morgan cooled off some, said casually, "Stranger . . . black man on a bay horse clubbed

Burt over the head. Dropped him like last week's newspaper.

"You get down there to Burt. Tell him to see the job gets done. I want that smart-alecky Ruby taken care of." Morgan pointed a stiff finger at Ashbel, his voice hard, demanding. "You tell Burt no more pussyfooting around. I want the job done, and I want it done right!"

Ashbel got to his feet, adjusted the swag of his pistol. Slamming a fist into the palm of his other hand, he begged, "Let me have him. You said next time." Ashbel threw back his rawhide vest flap, exposing a tin star. "I'll make it look right as rain."

Morgan eyed Ashbel coolly from where he had dropped down in the cushiony chair in back of his desk. Shoving back his chair, he said sagely, "Republicans are out on their ears now because they had badge-toters like you doing their killing. We've got to be smarter. You let Burt handle this."

Ashbel's eyes fell, registering disappointment. Morgan continued glibly, "You know, Ashbel, a good lawman would be curious about a stranger riding into town starting trouble." Morgan smiled shrewdly. "Fact is, a good lawman would send him on his way . . . or else."

Ashbel's eyes lit up. He pulled on his hat and adjusted it. "Sure thing, boss. And I won't miss." Ashbel hurried out the door.

Dan Ashbel was a puppet sheriff. He was thin, slack-shouldered, hawk-nosed. He had been a thirty-dollar-a-month cowpuncher on Morgan's ranch until Democrats took over the state and Morgan made him sheriff.

Morgan was a prominent Democrat. He had strong connections at the statehouse. He had prospered fast, handpicking his most reliable ranch hands for local offices to back him up.

Burt Lindley, the man who had been down in the street wearing the white hat, and the burly man, Mort Stall, were

Hamilton men, sent to whip up the crowd. During the commotion, Burt was to put a bullet in Ruby.

Morgan already knew that Governor Coke was going to sign an executive order disarming colored men, effective at the end of the month. Fact was, Morgan had pushed hard for the order, calling in all his political chips.

As freedmen without guns, they'd have to survive the white man's rule by brains and cunning, or submit. Unless they had a brainy man to lead them. And Morgan knew the only black man around capable of such was ex-senator George T. Ruby.

Morgan figured that with Ruby out of the way, coloreds could be molded into farm and ranch chattels this time. His plan was stalled momentarily. But Morgan was clever, ruthless. He strode hard-heeled over the town. Morgan's destiny was the town's.

Cole swung down from his horse at the wide doors of the livery, led the horse inside. The hostler, a thick, rawboned, middle-aged man, came toward him.

The stable was a long shotgun affair laid out running north to south, broken in the middle by a blacksmith's forge and a tack room. There was a row of stalls down each wall and a manger in back of each stall. At least a dozen stalls near the front were occupied.

The hostler looked sourly at Cole. "Something I can do for you?" he asked grouchily.

"Hay and grain," Cole answered.

The man looked at Cole, an ugly turn to his lips. "You want him hayed and grained, have at it. Empty stall's there, feed's yonder."

"Look, mister—"

"That'll be four bits. In advance."

Cole had no way of knowing what every black man in and

around Tubac knew about the hostler, Ran Johnson: Ran had been a Confederate cavalry sergeant. His mind was still fighting the war. He had never accepted the view that black men were now on the same footing with him. Wages be damned if it demanded him to serve blacks! In Ran's mind that was unthinkable.

But Cole had seen the likes of Ran Johnson before. Fact was, the country was full of Ran Johnsons.

Cole dug in his jeans pocket, came out jingling a fistful of coins. Casually tossing a coin to Ran, he announced, "I'll pick him up in the morning . . ."

Ran instinctively plucked the coin out of the air. Before he realized what had just happened, Cole said, ". . . unless I need him before then," and walked off, leading his horse toward a stall, leaving Ran standing there, his mind searching for an answer.

He found an empty stall, stripped off his saddle gear. Presently, the scrape of boot heels came to him. He stopped, looked up.

Three men stood at the head of the stall, sunlight spreading at their backs: Sheriff Ashbel, Mort Stall, and Burt Lindley. Ashbel said harshly, "You! Get out here!"

Cole had been around long enough to know this was trouble. He had expected it. But not this quickly. He looked out the corner of his eyes, quickly inspecting the place, looking for any way to even the score. The high-roofed stable was lit only by the light of day. Next to his horse was an empty stall, hay scattered over the floor.

Where was the hostler? At his back? Waiting to ambush him?

Cole shifted the empty feed bucket to his left hand, walking lazily toward the men standing in the doorway.

"That's him," Mort said softly out the side of his mouth.

"I'll settle with him now," Lindley promised, speaking of the whack over the head he had taken.

"We'll do this my way," Sheriff Ashbel told them.

Cole stopped six feet away, waiting.

Ashbel threw back his vest front, showing a tin badge. "Sheriff Ashbel. Your name?"

"Granger. Cole Granger."

"You got business here, Cole Granger? Or just passing through?"

"Passing through on business," Cole replied evenly.

"What business?"

"Hunting some horses. Blooded stock." Right there Cole caught the split-second sideward glance of Ashbel's eyes over to Mort's. Cole continued pleasantly, "Seems somebody wanted them horses bad enough to hang two Mexicans who stole 'em." He smiled thinly. "Saved me the job."

Ashbel was momentarily disconcerted, his train of thought thrown off track. This wasn't at all the way the conversation was supposed to go. "Who owned the horses?" he blurted.

"Mr. Driskill. MFD. But the hanging job would've fell to me. I was fetching 'em."

"Maybe you—"

"Let's git on with it!" Mort snapped impatiently. "We ain't got to listen to his life's story!" Mort lifted his left foot off the ground, stepping toward Cole. Mort was a big, heavy-footed, clumsy man. As his foot came down, Cole's left hand whipped out with the speed of a striking rattler. The feed bucket exploded alongside Mort's head, smashing him before he could take a step.

The unexpected blow drove Mort to his knees. And in one smooth motion, Cole's pistol came into his right hand.

Ashbel and Lindley were caught flat-footed. They both had on broadcloth suitcoats, only the tail ends of their holsters visible. There simply was nothing they could do.

Ashbel's face turned white, then red. "You throwin' down on me like that! There'll be hell to pay!"

"I come here looking for horses, not trouble. You brought it, not me."

"All the same, you're going to pay for this."

Suddenly a thin but commanding voice interrupted. "All right! Everybody just hold it right there!"

Cole had already seen the two men when they stepped off the boardwalk at the Exchange Hotel. Now the others twisted around, looking.

It was McNelly. Armstrong was with him.

McNelly's face was grim, tight-jawed. "Holster that gun!" he snapped. McNelly had spoken to Cole, but his eyes had been on Ashbel. "No use in me asking what this is about. You'd lie anyhow."

Ashbel stiffened but said nothing.

McNelly shifted his eyes from Ashbel to the other two men standing there. And McNelly didn't like what he saw. "Ashbel." McNelly said the name derisively, scornfully. "Marshal Ashbel," he said lightly. "Get hold of Morgan. Tell him Captain McNelly wants to see him. My headquarters are at the Exchange Hotel. The clerk'll tell him which room." McNelly's tone was dismissive.

Sheriff Ashbel didn't like taking orders, but he knew all local peace officers were under the authority of any state ranger.

Ashbel turned away meekly, hesitantly, sauntered off, looking back. Lindley and Mort followed.

McNelly was a tubercular man. Fitful spells of racking coughs would seize him unexpectedly. The slightest change in the air would chill him through. A heavy coat was his usual attire at night.

When they were gone McNelly lowered his head, both hands jammed in his coat pockets, thin lips puckered, eyes on the ground, his mind pondering his next course of action.

Presently he spoke, still studying the ground. "Armstrong, you see this nigger here?"

"Yes, sir," Armstrong answered, blinking.

"Come noon day after tomorrow, you see him, disarm him. He causes any more trouble before then, arrest him. He resist, shoot him." McNelly looked directly at Armstrong. "Any questions?"

"No sir, Capt'n."

McNelly turned, slouched off without a backward glance.

Chapter Seven

Boot heels swishing on the stairway caught the attention of the hotel clerk, who was lighting a coal-oil lamp in the far corner of the hotel lobby. He paused, listened momentarily, then lit the wick. Shaking out the match, he replaced the lamp globe.

"Yes, Mr. Hamilton?" the clerk asked down to the man who had just walked from the lobby to the bottom of the stairs.

"You got a Captain McNelly registered, Lynus?"

"Yes sir. Him and his men got two rooms. Five and six. The captain's in six."

"Thank you, Lynus."

A moment later, Morgan stood poised at the door to room 6, gathering his thoughts. Abruptly, he rapped sharply.

"Who is it?" a weak voice asked from inside.

"Morgan Hamilton."

"Door's open," the weak voice answered.

Morgan came in, eyes taking in the paucity of the unlit room.

McNelly was sitting slump-shouldered on a field cot against the wall, his feet on the floor, a heavy wool blanket draped over his thin shoulders.

"Excuse my manners," McNelly said. "Night air don't sit well with me no more."

"Captain McNelly?"

McNelly's cold eyes held Hamilton's. "Don't look like much, do I?" Before Hamilton could answer, McNelly straightened his shoulders, said with authority, "I'm Leander McNelly, Captain, Texas Rangers."

"Why'd you want to see me?"

"Citizens been complaining to the statehouse about the lawlessness in Tubac. They profess no confidence in the local law to protect 'em, look after their property."

"What's that got to do with me, Captain?"

"You're a big man around here. Got lots of pull at the statehouse." McNelly's breath started to come heavy. He raised a fist to his white lips, coughed three rapid body-racking coughs.

Morgan couldn't have cared less. He just stood there, disinterested, a bland look on his face. Now Morgan could relax. This frail man was no threat to his plans.

McNelly cleared his throat, continued, "See that book over yonder," and pointed. "Every man in the county that's outside the law is in that book. Including you."

Hamilton stiffened. "I'm a law-abiding rancher! You got nothing on me!"

"Put that book together myself some years back. Even back then you was outlaw. That's how you built your ranch, how you got good stock."

"You can't prove that!" Morgan snapped.

"Morgan, I'm goin' to say it once, and only once. Cattle rustling and horse thieving is over. Any man missing stock

90

will report to the authority. Any outfit lynching and killing over disputed beeves will be treated as outlaws. You got hired gunmen, disband them. Send them out of the county.''

"Now see here, Captain, you got no right—''

"You got objections, take it up with the statehouse!'' McNelly snapped.

Morgan fell silent, turning the brim of his Stetson in his fingers. Directly he turned, headed toward the door.

McNelly said at his back, "Morgan, I might not look like much, but you take my words as gospel. I'll see you hang if you so much as look the wrong way.''

The moon was pale in the west, the sky slate-gray with the coming of dawn. Cole stuck a toe in the stirrup, swung onto the saddle. He walked the bay out of the livery where he had slept the night before. At the end of the street he swung south where the unusual tracks of the Andalusians led.

It was midmorning when Cole topped out on a low-rolling hill and pulled to a halt.

He had been following the tracks all morning. Had already crossed the Big Sands, a six-mile swath of ankle-deep sandy earth grown over with mesquite, scrub oak, and briars. He had waded Los Olmos creek, followed south down Sabinal Draw for a mile or so. He had seen only about fifty head of beeves, all wearing Box H brand. The country had already been picked clean of stock, nothing at all in the way of riding stock. His horses had simply vanished. The tracks literally washed out.

It was in Cole's mind that wherever those horses were, they would surely be pinned up. They were too valuable to let graze free like most range ponies.

A ranch. A well-guarded ranch. Cole figured that's where they'd be.

Off in the distance was a lovely green valley. Fifty acres at least. Sheltered by rolling hills on each side. The sparkle of a stream running through it from north to south.

He rode down off the hill.

A ways off to the north, the clear blue sky had a smudge on it. He stood in his stirrups, straining his eyes for distance.

And there it was!

A ranch house, snugged back in the notch of two hills, a lazy tendril of smoke curling away from the chimney.

He dropped back down in the saddle, headed that way.

It was a ranch house, all right. It had a shotgun-style bunkhouse off to the side, and a hay barn with a pole corral set back a ways. At least a dozen horses were grazing inside the corral.

He walked his horse along the brow of the hill, keeping to the shadows, his eyes searching the ranch yard for sign of life. A scattering of chickens pecked away in back of the hay barn. A horse lifted its head, sniffing the wind.

It was a fabulous setup. By the looks of the place Cole knew it could only be Morgan Hamilton's ranch, the Box H.

It had plenty of graze and running water; the house was constructed of native stone with four heavy colonial columns. A wide veranda fronted the place.

And there in with the rest of the fine horses were the two Andalusians!

Cole felt sure Morgan had men who drew fighting wages. And Morgan was not a man foolish with his money. The men he hired would kill.

Cole drew up in a cluster of pecan trees, studying the layout.

Nobody was in sight. Nothing stirred.

Nothing unusual about that, Cole thought. All hands would be out on the range. But the boss is rarely left completely alone. Someone else had to be around.

This was on Cole's mind as he studied the layout.

A thought came to mind, took hold, grew.

He dismounted, stripped saddle gear from his horse, picketed him on good grass close to the creek. Quickly he dabbed water from his canteen under his armpits, then poured some down his back exactly where a man would sweat. Loosening his shellbelt a notch, he slouched his gun toward his hip pocket, tugging the belt down low across his hips, looking slouchy, indifferent.

Taking his Winchester in his right hand, he slung his saddle gear across his left shoulder and walked away from the creek, toward the ranch house.

He was almost to the barn when a white man appeared. He was medium-built, average height, had his sleeves rolled up, a gun slung around his waist. He saw Cole. Stopped. Shoved back his hat to the crown of his head, put his hands on his hips, watching Cole come on.

Cole kept coming, dragging his feet like a man ready to collapse from a long walk. Twenty feet off, Cole spoke. "Mornin', suh," he said, drawling deferentially, head down.

"Looks like you been walking some," the white man said.

"Yeah, suh, I have. That old mule of mine plumb played out on me back yonder." Cole smiled broadly. "He wadn't no 'count nohow." He dropped the saddle at his feet, shifted the Winchester nonchalantly to his other hand, eyes searching over the place all the time. "Sho' could use somethin' to ride. I can buy or borry."

"Well . . . if you got money you can take it up with the boss. If you ain't got money, don't bother."

"Man wouldn't offer to buy unless he had money," Cole answered, smiling knowingly.

"That's right. A man wouldn't," the white man retorted dryly.

"Who the boss?"

"Mr. Hamilton."

Suddenly Cole and the white man flinched. Gunfire!

93

Drumming hoofbeats, loud yahooing. More gunfire.

Cole and the white man hit the dirt, scrambled behind the water trough there next to the corral.

Seven riders swooped down out of the hill from the east, pistols blazing, every man yelling like mad. They jerked to a wild, ragged stop at the back of the corral. A vaquero snaked a rope over a corral post, spurred his horse backward, pulling out a section of fence. The other vaqueros lashed their horses through the opening.

Quick as a man could blink, a dozen prize horses were driven from the corral.

Including the Andalusians!

The vaqueros had worked with skill, precision. But before they pulled out, Cole got a glimpse of the leader. Rudolpho.

The white man had kept his head down. When the thieves first struck, it took him a while to grasp what was happening. He only got off one shot. His pistol had banged, a hail of bullets zinged in at him, kicking up dirt around the water trough. When he peeped out from the other end of the trough, Cole had recognized Rudolpho.

Now the white man stood up, his gun held carelessly at his side. His face was ashen, his voice derisive. "You sorry no-'count! . . ." The white man's voice changed, became exasperated. "Damn greasers ride in here, make off with the boss's prize horses, and you don't have the guts to lift a finger." Pointing at Cole's Winchester, he screamed angrily, "What you got that thing for?"

Cole stood up, hefted the Winchester, keeping his finger on the action, the muzzle generally on the white man. "This?" Cole asked, smiling. "This just for rattlesnakes and—"

A screen door slammed.

A tall man leaped off the porch, came at a dead run, a Winchester held in his two hands.

Cole knew it was Morgan Hamilton. He jacked a round in

the chamber. At the sharp click, the eyes of the white man next to him got big.

Cole swung the barrel at his belly.

The man dropped his pistol.

"That wasn't my fight," Cole said. "But this is."

Morgan saw what had happened. He came to a stumbling walk, his mind comprehending.

"Hold it right there," Cole ordered Morgan. "Drop the rifle!"

Morgan stopped and threw the Winchester away from his body. "You again. You have a hand in this?"

"Not the way you think. I came to get my horses. But somebody beat me to 'em."

"Your horses? You're crazy! That was all prime stock."

"Maybe you already did own prize horses. How you come by them others is none of my business. But two days ago two stolen claybank duns was turned into that corral. I come to get 'em."

Morgan's face turned red. "I'll kill even a white man for accusing me of being a horse thief. Unless you use that Winchester now, you'll hear from me!"

"That ain't likely," Cole said. "I seen men like you before, Mr. Hamilton. And if I got you pegged right, you hire your killing."

Morgan's cool blue eyes stabbed out at Cole, his thin lips tight. Morgan was being held at bay, and he didn't like it. But there was no give in him, just cold detached reality. "You want them horses," he said coolly, "they're out there." Morgan smiled wryly. "Go get them, black boy . . . and good riddance!"

"I aim to do just that," Cole said.

Cole gestured at the other man with his rifle barrel, moving him over where he could keep both of them covered.

Cole worked hastily. Scooping up the other man's pistol, he jammed it into his waistband. Retrieving Morgan's Winchester, barrel first, he whacked it bluntly against the ground, the stock parting from the barrel. He flung the barrel across the yard.

"You won't get away with this!" Morgan growled.

"I want no trouble with you. Just them horses." Pointing his rifle at Morgan's belly, he announced, "My horse is yonder," and he nodded. "You move before I get there, I'll kill you." He shouldered his saddle and, holding his Winchester in his right hand pistol fashion, walked backward away from the yard, checking over his shoulder every few steps.

At the bank of the creek the bay turned his head to Cole, flicked his ears forward. Working hastily, Cole threw the blanket and saddle on the bay, then stepped a toe in the stirrup.

When Cole splashed across Coyote Creek, the last he had seen was Morgan Hamilton and that other white man standing in the ranch yard. Hamilton had both hands on his hips. But Morgan was a cunning man, a man who wouldn't sit still for being outdone.

Now Morgan looked at the white man standing there next to him and said, "Drake, drive up some range horses, then ride out to the east range and tell Harley and the boys what happened. You tell Harley it was them same Mexicans from across the river. Tell him to take enough of the boys to get them horses back. And teach them greasers a lesson."

"Yes sir, Mr. Hamilton."

"And Drake."

"Yes sir?"

"Tell Harley about that nigger what was here. I want him dead!"

GET YOUR 4 FREE BOOKS NOW—
A VALUE BETWEEN $16 AND $20

Mail the Free Book Certificate Today!

FREE BOOKS CERTIFICATE!

YES! I want to subscribe to the Leisure Western Book Club. Please send my 4 FREE BOOKS. Then, each month, I'll receive the four newest Leisure Western Selections to preview FREE for 10 days. If I decide to keep them, I will pay the Special Members Only discounted price of just $3.36 each, a total of $13.44. This saves me between $3 and $6 off the bookstore price. There are no shipping, handling or other charges. There is no minimum number of books I must buy and I may cancel the program at any time. In any case, the 4 FREE BOOKS are mine to keep—at a value of between $17 and $20! Offer valid only in the USA.

Name_____

Address_____

City_____ State_____

Zip_____ Phone_____

Biggest Savings Offer!

For those of you who would like to pay us in advance by check or credit card—we've got an even bigger savings in mind. Interested? Check here. ☐

If under 18, parent or guardian must sign.
Terms, prices and conditions subject to change. Subscription subject to acceptance. Leisure Books reserves the right to reject any order or cancel any subscription.

GET FOUR BOOKS TOTALLY *FREE*—A VALUE BETWEEN $16 AND $20

Chapter Eight

Jim Seely and Mike Driskill sat their horses at the edge of the rimrock, looking down on the ragged circle of Studebaker wagons in the broad valley.

Nothing further could be done about Cole now. Ranch work waited for no man.

Seely was slumped lazily in his saddle, his two hands stacked on the saddle horn, his hat pushed back on the crown of his head. He saw nothing threatening about the wagons stopped on MFD range. It happened all the time.

But Mike was having none of it. He sat alert in the saddle, a solid-built youngster, jaws tight, reins held poised, ready to spur his horse into action.

"What we sittin' here for, Jim? Let's make 'em hit the trail. Same as Pa would do!"

"Mike, I ain't so sure that's what your pa would do," the older man said, concealing his annoyance at Mike's callousness.

97

"Pa sent squatters packin' before. These ain't no different!"

Seely turned, looking across his shoulder at Mike, and said patiently, "There's a difference. Maybe you just don't see it."

"Only difference is they're niggers," Mike said. "And that's all the more reason."

"Maybe you don't think so, but they're human too," Jim said flatly. "They come onto troubles same as anybody." Seely drew himself up in the saddle. "I don't know what's eatin' you since this Cole trouble. Stompin' down other people don't raise a man taller."

"You sayin' we let 'em stay?"

"I figure this ain't for neither one of us to say. I'll send word back to Frank." Seely swung his horse, cantered off.

Mike sat his horse there a minute or two, looking. Seething. Suddenly he wrenched his horse around, spurred out, galloping after Seely.

A lone cowhand galloped his horse up to the hitchrail in front of the ranch house and swung down from the saddle. Removing his hat, he wiped sweat from the band, used the hat to slap dust from his faded jeans. Stepping up onto the porch, he rapped on the doorjamb, then put his back to the door, waiting.

From inside, boot heels scraped across the floor. A mild voice sounded through the screen. "Rolly? That you?"

"It's me, boss."

"Cole?" Driskill asked hopefully.

"No sir."

"What you doin' here, then?" Frank Driskill pushed out the screen door, stepped out onto the porch.

"Jim sent me. We got squatters on the west range."

"Jim knows what the rules are. Send 'em packin'!"

"These are different, boss. Niggers. And they got troubles. Jim figured you ought to handle it."

Frank swore. "Bring my horse," he ordered Rolly. Then he swore some more.

Five men—Frank and Mike Driskill, Jim Seely, and two other cowhands, Ramon and Henry—arrived back at the lip of the canyon, sitting their horses in a ragged line, their eyes taking in the scene below.

Six canvas-covered wagons were loosely bunched just off from a copse of pecan trees, a finger of smoke trailing up from a campfire. And four people, three men and a woman, milled about the fire.

Seely repeated what he had already told Frank, "Not a single head of stock in sight, Frank. They couldn't push on soon even if they wanted to."

Frank swore again softly, then said gently to Mike, "We get down there, you hold your tongue. Let me do the talkin'."

Mike was silent. Everybody knew Mike had no use for colored people, for whatever reason.

Frank's eyes held Mike's, demanding an answer. Finally Mike said grudgingly, "All right, Pa."

Frank spurred the blue roan. Over the rim he plunged, down the canyon wall he galloped, heading for the camp.

At the edge of the wagons, Frank pulled up sharply.

A black man.

Frank wheeled the roan, faced him.

Mike wheeled his horse, joined Frank's side. Seely and the rest of the men drew up on both sides.

The black man was tall, thin-waisted, deep-brown complexion, chocolate-colored. In his early thirties. His mouth was big, like a long gash stretching from ear to ear. He had a brand-new Winchester in his two hands, a pistol slung low around his waist. He was standing spread-legged off from the wagons as though he was ready to fight. Two rifle barrels were sticking out from behind the tailgate of one of the wagons.

"Howdy. Name's Frank Driskill. Seen your smoke."

"How do. Tyree Woods. Y'all welcome. Coffee's makin'."

"Smells mighty good. Smelled it all the way up on the rimrock." Driskill deliberately rose in his saddle, twisted around looking, talking casually all the while. "Where you people headed?"

"Californy."

Driskill dismounted slowly, with effort, palming his reins. The rest of the men got down too.

"Mr. Woods," said Driskill, smiling, "California will likely be floating out in the ocean by the time you people get there. You ain't got a head of stock in sight." Driskill shifted his tone, said soberly, "Indians run off your stock, did they?"

Tyree's shoulders sagged. The arms holding the Winchester went limp. "They come on us last night," he said resignedly. "Night guard never heard nothin'. They ran off twenty-four mules and four horses."

"Uh-huh," Frank grunted knowingly. "You ain't the first. Indians make a livin' at it. They'll steal the horse you ridin' if you ain't watchful." Frank said over his shoulder to his riders, "Coffee smells good, boys. Let's see how it tastes." Frank and Tyree exchanged looks, and both men headed toward the fire. Frank asked Tyree on the way, "South of here the way y'all come, you didn't happen to hear of or see a young feller named Cole . . . Cole Granger, did you?"

"Can't say I did."

"Didn't expect you did, but thought I'd ask. What you folks plan on doin'?"

"At first light my best man took to the trail of them Indians."

"That's as good a way as any to get a man killed," Frank said mildly. "Them Indians ain't likely to be awed by one man on foot."

Tyree chuckled. "I know a good bit about Indians. This ain't the first bunch I piloted through. My thinkin' is, if we get lucky, one of them mules or maybe a horse will break away from the rest. Jesse could spot him a mile off out there on the prairie."

Frank had already taken a cup of coffee from a thin, dark-skinned woman who was tending the fire. Now he raised his tin cup to his lips, took a sip, lowered the cup. "Best not to trust to luck when it comes to Indians."

Frank said to one of his hands, "Ramon, they got a man gone. Take a look out there, see what you can find. Take Henry's horse with you just in case."

Mike stiffened, mad at what Frank was doing. He had already gotten halfway mad when his father ask Tyree about Cole. This was too much for him to take. His coffee cup froze in midair on the way to his lips. "Pa, we ain't—"

Frank brought his head around sharply, looking at Mike, a cold stare that reminded Mike that he had ageed to be quiet down here.

Mike shut up.

"And Ramon," Frank said finally, "stay clear of them Indians. You come up on Jesse, get the both of you back here. You come up on any stock, drive them in. Understand?"

"*Sí*, senor."

Frank turned back to Tyree. "My son there," he nodded at Mike, "sometimes lets youth rule his head."

"He ain't the first one," Tyree said. "Anyhow, we obliged to you."

Frank lifted his eyes along the thin trail of dust Ramon

was kicking up, leading the other horse. "Indians will stop and eat one or two of them mules. Scatter the rest. Warrior wouldn't be caught dead on a mule. They steal 'em just for show."

Mike was sitting on his heels tight-lipped next to the fire, his coffee cup still half full, a sour look on his face. He felt lost, out of place. So he just sat, listening to Henry, who had struck up a conversation with one of the black men. The black man was saying, "We found George 'fo daylight this mornin'. Deader'n a doorknob. Arrow in his chest. The horses gone."

"Them's Indian ways," Henry said. "You folks lucky. In a manner of speakin'. Indians got time they'll kill everybody, maybe torture a man, rape a woman. You got strong children, they'll take 'em. Make Indians out of 'em."

"We mighty lucky you folks come along. No tellin' how long we'd a been sittin' here."

Mike was irritated by the conversation. He rudely dashed his coffee into the flames, spewing up a shower of ashes and a plume of smoke.

Jim Seely looked consolingly at Mike. "Your pa's got his reasons, Mike."

"What reasons?" Mike snapped.

"These folks stranded! They got no other way!"

"They was doin' just fine before we came along."

Seely sighed impatiently. "Mike, you just can't get it through your head. These people are human just like white people. Why, if these were white people, you'd be the first to lend a hand."

Mike leaped to his feet like a mashed cat. "I got nothin' else to say on it!" Whirling, Mike hurled the cup away from his body, walked quickly away from the fire toward his horse. He mounted up, lashed his horse out of there without a backward glance.

Frank had watched it all; the hissing flames had gotten his

attention. Now Frank looked a question at Seely.

"He's hot under the collar, boss," Seely answered. "Figures you ought to leave these people to their doin'." Seely dashed the leavings of his coffee into the fire. "I best go talk to Mike," he announced.

Two hours went by. Ramon rode in with Jesse.

Frank Driskill was sleeping on his back under a pecan tree, his head resting on a saddle, his hat tipped over his eyes. He and Tyree had talked themselves out, ate some fried sidemeat and skillet-made corn bread, talked some more, and drank some more coffee. Finally Frank decided to loosen the cinch on his saddle and doze some.

Now the clatter of approaching hoofbeats woke him up. He drew his legs under him, stood up.

At the sight of Jesse, Frank asked Ramon, "Any sign of the stock?"

"*Sí,* senor. We drove them there in the draw." Ramon pointed. "It is a good place. They will stay."

"How far?" Tyree asked.

"Just around the bend," Jesse answered. "In a feeder draw. We got nineteen mules. Saw where the Indians butchered two. The other mules and the horses nowhere in sight."

Tyree smiled happily and announced loudly to the people standing watching Ramon and Jesse. "All right, folks! We got our teams back! Prepare to move out!" Tyree turned to Driskill. "Much obliged for everything, mister. You saved our bacon."

Driskill looked at Ramon, asked dubiously, "You sure they'll have no trouble gettin' them mules to the wagons?"

"*Sí,* senor. No trouble."

Driskill put his hat on, tugged the brim down. "Well, luck to you folks," he said to Tyree.

Tyree was standing off to the side when Driskill swung onto the saddle, kneed the roan around, and said, "I'll have

the boys drive in three, four cow ponies. You'll need 'em."
And Driskill spurred out.

Far to the east in the statehouse at Austin, the twelfth
session of the state legislature was just adjourning. Democrats had been in complete control, enjoying a majority of
18 to 12 in the Senate and 61 to 29 in the House. And they
had used their majority to great advantage, turning back Republican acts that had enfranchised and protected freedmen.

Senator Ruby was completely nullified, a broken man
now. And so was Senator Matthew Gaines, the other black
member of the Senate. Now there were no voices left to
speak up on behalf of the black man; white Republicans had
their own political bacon to look after.

It had been a bitter, rancorous twelfth session.

Senator Ruby had made an impassioned appeal for justice
and fair play. But his words had been met by turned ears,
catcalls, and threats of retaliation. Amid shouted boos and
whistles of derision, the Speaker, Ira Campbell, gaveled the
session adjourned. Elated Democratics scattered, each going
his own way to make political capital out of having control
of the state again.

Two men stayed behind, sitting alone in the empty Senate
chamber, talking in low voices.

The heavyset, medium-height man was Senator John Mullis, a purse-proud vain man. Mullis was a smooth politician
of surpassing skills. He had a quick mind tied to a glib
tongue.

The other man was Zell Biggers. Zell was nothing more
than a mewling conniver, a political hanger-on and word-
carrier for Morgan Hamilton.

Mullis was saying, "Republicans are up in arms over this
order to disarm coloreds. Ruby and Gaines are railing against
it. I wouldn't low-rate Ruby's chances."

"What can Ruby do? Governor Coke already promised to sign the measure," Biggers said indifferently.

"We mustn't underestimate Ruby," Mullis said thoughtfully. "He knows the state police is rife with colored Republicans. It'll take careful planning to take weapons out of their hands. It won't be done easily."

Mullis cocked his head, said reflectively, "But suppose a colored policeman was to be involved again in a killing or two?"

"There'd be hell to pay," Biggers said.

"Right. The vigilantes might even get involved. Raise hob, maybe commit a lynching in retaliation. Or maybe go on a wild mob rampage.

"Ruby would report the lawlessness to Washington," Mullis said, smiling.

"The federal government coming in?" Biggers asked in disbelief.

"That's right," Mullis said. "But this time on our side. With exaggerated tales of mass atrocities against white people by the state police, they'll have to come in on our side."

"It could happen," Mullis said. "We won't have this thing in our hip pockets untill the state police is disbanded."

"Seems simple enough for the governor to just issue the order, then get every sheriff to enforce it."

"Every sheriff ain't on our side. That'll take time. And time ain't on our side in this matter." The senator drew up attentively in his seat. "Another thing, the railroad act didn't pass. The governor couldn't deliver the goods."

Biggers's eyebrows lifted. "Why?"

"Price was too steep. Not a man in the legislature was willing to vote the Texas and Pacific Railroad twenty-four sections of land for each mile of track laid over the proposed route. The best the governor could finagle was a compromise for a shorter route. Tubac is out. The majority of senators think Tubac has no future."

"No future?" Biggers asked incredulously. "The town's growing by leaps and bounds. Faster'n any other."

"No Democratic future," Senator Mullis said flatly. "See that Morgan gets the word. He'll want to know as soon as possible."

"This'll break Morgan. He had his aim set high for Tubac."

"Morgan knew them eastern men were Republicans. They'll not stretch a railroad where it'll do Democrats good. See that Morgan hears the whole of it."

"This'll play hob with Morgan's ambitions."

"Morgan ain't the only one who staked a future in that railroad coming through Tubac. There's no help for it."

The sun was casting long shadows over Tubac's main street when Morgan Hamilton rode in on a gimlet-hammed, narrow-chested range pony. All his good horses had been stolen.

Morgan swung down, rudely threw a hasty cinch knot over the hitchrail. He was mad. All the way into town the rank-broke range horse had given Morgan nothing but trouble, pitching and bucking, fighting the bit.

Morgan's boot heels rang going across the boardwalk, and he shoved through the door at the Exchange Hotel.

Lynus lifted his eyes from the newspaper he was reading, saw who it was, said hastily, "Telegram for you, Mr. Hamilton."

Morgan took the telegram and ascended the stairs to his second-story room, reading the wire even as he went. In front of the door to his room as he inattentively searched his pocket for the key, the full impact of what the telegram said hit him. Morgan froze, focused his attention, took in the words carefully: TUBAC LOST OUT STOP RAILROAD TO EXTEND WESTWARD STOP PLAN ACCORDINGLY STOP.

Morgan's mind swirled. His carefully laid plans had gone

down the drain. Without the railroad Tubac would dry up, slip back into a wasteland, nothing but another high prairie blot on the arid land where tumbleweeds blew and rattlesnakes nested.

Morgan shoved the key into the keyhole, turned it, shoved through the door, hung his hat on a peg there. He started pacing the room, retracing his steps like a penned-up wolf. Directly Morgan slowed down, lifted a hand to his chin, stroked it thoughtfully. Slowly his face spread red, lips drew tight. Then he whirled, hurled the wadded telegram against the far wall.

Morgan knew there was only one ranchman west of Tubac big enough to command the attention of the railroad bosses.

Frank Driskill.

Morgan ran his fingers through his wavy hair, swore softly, bitterly, then said through gritted teeth, "Frank Driskill . . . I'll ruin you for this!"

Chapter Nine

The Mexican horse thieves rode in a great hurry, pushing the stolen horses hard, ahead of Cole an hour at most.

And Cole was riding hard too.

He had swept around the fringes of Big Sands, had ridden up to Los Olmos Creek where the horses had been watered, then driven on across.

Now Cole sat in the saddle, his horse drinking. Straining back on the reins, he lifted the horse's dripping muzzle.

Wading the bay across, he easily found the tracks of the horse herd, the big hoofprints of the Andalusians still rimmed dark with dripped water. He booted the bay into a gallop, closing the distance.

After a while the land turned to low flat-topped hills, stark limestone ledges, dotted with hulking prickly pear topped off with red and yellow pear apples. The air was clean, scented from green scrub cedar.

He galloped on, the bay choosing his way, going through

tall stalks of sotol, holly-thorned agarita bushes, sacahuiste grass.

Then the land broke, a gravely swath: Sabinal Draw. He scrambled the horse across the shallow draw, checked down to a shambling trot, held it.

Directly the trail led down off the low divide, switched back into a dry wash, skirting the outer fringes of a broad mesquite flat. The tracks of the horse herd were fresh now, awfully fresh. Newly turned stones were dark on one side. Moisture. Catclaw grass was still slumped over, trampled by the horse herd.

He slowed down, riding warily now, eyes reaching out for movement, ears alert for sound.

Nothing on the mesquite flat grew taller than a man on horseback. But this was a good place for a man to lie in ambush.

He pulled to a halt, scouting the terrain.

The place was nothing more than a stand of stunted trees, three acres at most, crudely oval-shaped. Looked like there was a runoff draw or dry wash on the north side.

He swung his horse quietly, headed that way.

Halfway through the trees he cut sign of the horse herd. The tracks still headed south. The blurred hoofprints of the Andalusians were there.

But something didn't look right. Ambush, maybe.

He backtracked through the dry wash, skirted the trees in a rough circles, searching for movement in the trees.

He had swung almost south when he saw the finger of water, standing out stark against the ridged and gashed landscape. And just at the edge of the water a small settlement. Two cracker-box-size adobe buildings and a dugout. Off to the side of the dugout was a ferry crossing.

Cole came on, walking the bay down the narrow road running in front of the buildings. Nothing stirred. Nobody in sight. The hoofprints of the horse herd had played out in the hard-packed earth.

The corner of his eye caught the bleached sign in front of the first adobe: CHANCEY'S SALOON.

Three horses stood, heads bowed, at the hitchrail. A dog was lying by the wall in a rectangle of shade. It was hot, very hot. Heat reflected off the buildings, doubly hot.

He guided the bay to the hitchrail, swung down, looking around.

The saloon had no doors, just a wide gape where doors ought to have been. He walked forward, taking the thong off his pistol. He stopped in the open doorway, looking around inside.

Three men—two white, one Mexican—were seated at a table over in the corner. Hearing the jingle of Cole's spurs, all three looked up. The bartender stopped wiping the bar and looked up too.

One of the white men had his back to the wall, facing Cole. He was tall, wide-shouldered, looked to be in his late twenties. He had a dull-gray hat tipped back on his head, showing all of his deep-tanned face. Staring out at Cole, he lifted his mug deliberately, downed the last of his beer. With calculated ease he turned up the pitcher, poured himself another, his eyes on Cole all the time. Directly he spoke conversationally to the man sitting next to him. "Our luck done plumb played out, Will."

Will Dancer was a big stoop-shouldered man. He had a seamed, sun-wrinkled face. His hat was lying on the table next to him. A shock of red hair was plastered down to his head from the heat. "How's that?" Will answered innocently.

"Wind's just blowed more trash our way."

Will took the cue. He said to the Mexican at the table, "Juan, you smell somethin' the wind just blowed in?"

The thin-faced, slight-built Mexican looked out at Cole

110

from under his big sombrero, smiling crookedly. "*Sí*, senor. The smell of something dead."

Now, Cole had seen a lot of one-horse towns, and had been taunted before. Loafers, tail-enders, troublemakers he had put up with before. He had been up the trail before. But now he was hot, tired, and thirsty. And this taunting struck him with an ugly bite to it.

"Beer," Cole said, flipping a two-bit piece on the bar. "Beer."

The bartender turned to go, but not before looking vaguely over in the corner. A warning, Cole thought. Or fear.

"You a mite off the trail, ain't you, boy?" the tall, wide-shouldered man said.

Cole ignored the man and took up the beer the bartender had just slid over to him.

"Guess he don't hear too well, Kelly," the other white man said, a twisted smile on his lips. "Maybe you better tell him again."

Kelly smiled at Will's urging. He said out loud to Cole, "Niggers don't usually stop here. Place's a little too quick for 'em," he added, and grinned at his own wit.

Cole looked over at the bartender, asked loudly enough for them to hear, "Senor, you got a sheriff here?"

All three of the men over at the table guffawed at Cole's obviously silly question. There wasn't a lawman within a hundred miles of the place.

"No, senor," the barkeep said. "No sheriff."

"That's too bad," Cole said, calmly setting his beer down. "I figured somebody would want to know when a nigger kill a white man . . . Mexican too, maybe."

"But, senor . . ."

Cole faced around to the three men at the table even as the bartender was speaking. "But then again, I don't guess anybody cares about killing a snake . . . unless it's another snake."

111

The smile left Kelly's lips, and his face went white. Will and Juan both stiffened. They knew this stranger was just asking to be shot dead.

Kelly rudely shoved back his chair from the table, jumped up, kicked the chair backward away from him. "That's mighty brave talk," he snarled. "Let's see you back it up!"

"Take my word on it, mister," Cole said quietly. "This gun I'm wearing ain't for show. You'll have lead in you before you clear leather."

"The hell you preach!"

Cole's gun hand swept down the split second Kelly's shoulder moved forward, and his fingers came up gripping the Walker Colt. The muzzle flamed, flamed again. The first slug slammed into Kelly's holster just as Kelly's hand gripped his gun butt. The dull *whump* of lead on blue steel sent shock waves through Kelly's fist. He snatched his hand away, stunned. Pain leaped up his elbow. Cole's next shot shattered the half-empty pitcher of beer on the table. Shards of glass flew, beer cascaded down on the table, dousing the other two men sitting there.

Outside the horses jerked their heads up, startled by gunfire. The mangy dog lying in the shade bolted to his feet, ran off to find a safer resting place.

The Mexican instinctively whirled around in his chair, poised his gun hand. Will had stood up halfway, crouching over the table, his gun hand ready to draw.

"No use in dying over him," Cole said coldly. "I'd just as soon walk outa here same as I walked in."

The Mexican's gun hand went slack, fell away. Will looked questioningly over at Kelly. The bartender was frozen in his tracks, jaw dropped.

Cole said to Will, still looking at Kelly, "He ain't got nothin' else to say. He already talked too much."

Will's body slumped. He sank back down in his chair.

Cole looked at Kelly. "Like you said, town's too quick

for me. I'm leaving." He backstepped to the doorway. "I'll pull myself across the ferry. You boys have another drink while I'm at it."

The shift of the state from Republican to Democratic rule threw the political climate into turmoil. Tolerance for another man's views was thrown to the wind. Disputes were settled with guns. Old animosities were dug up and rehashed. Revenge was the name of the game. Payback was vicious and sometimes terminal.

Two colored state policemen were hanged on trumped-up charges of cattle rustling. A white man accused of having been a scalawag, a Southern man with Unionist leanings during the war, was run out of the country.

And on and on.

Democrats retaliated. Some Republican bigwigs got out of the country for good. Valid and invalid wrongdoings of the past administration were editorialized on, inciting retribution. The caustic editor of the *San Antonio Register,* a Democratic organ, let loose with a hard-hitting, slanderous editorial, ending thusly:

"Shriek not at the defeat of the Republican party. That crowd of despots are known everywhere as the party of carpetbaggers, scalawags, and nigger lovers, and is despised by all right-thinking white men. Now they rush to the statehouse, pleading the case of the colored man like a father would a son's. One need not wonder why this is so!"

Every Democrat newspaper picked up the editorial and reprinted it for local agitation. Some Republicans cringed in horror at the blunt suggestion; others stiffened with fight. Colored men sagged in despair.

Democrats gloated at the stinging gibe.

Morgan Hamilton had the the *Tubac Ledger* folded under his arm, walking briskly, a spring to his step, a pleasant turn

113

to his lips. He turned into the door of the newspaper office, searched for the editor, found him.

Morgan started talking the moment he walked through the batwings, holding up the paper to the editor. "Olny, this piece you got in here interests me. I'd like a word with you about it."

Olny Matthews was a little squeaky-voiced man of middle age. He was a loose-working man, in the business strictly for money. He had recently abandoned Santa Angela because he had lost out on the new printing contract.

Olny straightened up from his printing press where he had been setting type, wiped his ink-smeared hands on his green apron, looking out at Morgan from under a green eyeshade.

"Democrats are out for scalps," Olny said, smiling. "Figured my readers ought to know."

"You know the man who wrote this piece?"

"Sal McMahan over at the *San Antonio Register*. Been there for years. And he's got years of Republican hate stored up in his pen, too."

"This last paragraph," Morgan indicated, "you think he knows somethin', or just spoutin' off?"

"I've knowed Sal eight, ten years. He's a good newspaperman. The best. When Sal goes to print, you can bet your bottom dollar he's got facts."

"You sayin' he's got names to put to this accusation?"

"I'd bet my last on it." Olny smiled wryly. "Man comes right out and say a white man got nigger children, he better have names. And a gun, too."

Morgan smiled, his eyes twinkling at the prospects. "How long you been here now, Olny? Six . . . seven months?"

"Going on six months, Mr. Hamilton."

"I could make your stay here long and pleasant." Morgan's eyes narrowed with sinister delight. "And profitable."

Olny cocked his eyebrows. "You want names?"

"You read my mind, Olny," Morgan said graciously.

There was discernible white blood in scores of colored people; this was indisputable. Where the white blood came from was a matter for speculation by some, a damaging blot on the honor of others. It was a subject kept away from public talk by white people. Now it had been laid out in the open like a busted blister. A lot of white men were in pain.

Mike Driskill sat in a hide-bottomed chair at the end of a long crude table running the length of the bunkhouse nursing a scalding hot cup of coffee, eyes riveted on the newspaper spread out in front of him, lips mouthing the words.

Jim Seely downed the last of his coffee, got up from the bench at the table, stepped over to the sheet-iron stove, and lifted the coffeepot, pouring himself another. Jim glanced up casually at Mike, then took up his filled cup, walked back over to the table. Dropping down on the bench, Jim glanced at Mike again. The frown that had been on Jim's brow since Mike picked up the newspaper deepened.

Jim picked up a dog-eared magazine, leafed through it, deliberately rustling the pages. He glanced at Mike once more.

Mike's face was flushed white, jaws set.

Jim closed the pages loudly, casually tossed the magazine in the center of the table. "Must be mighty interestin' readin' you run across there. You ain't lifted your head in twenty minutes."

"Uh-huh," Mike grunted without lifting his eyes.

The latest newspaper and a stack of old dog-eared magazines were always in the bunkhouse. Jim had already gone over the newspaper this morning, as all other hands who could read had done. Jim knew exactly what was holding Mike's attention. The same as it had done the others'.

"Political sermonizin'?" Jim asked Mike conversationally.

Mike carefully folded the newspaper, straightened up to

Jim, his eyes blank. "Uh-huh. Mighty touchy words there, too. I never thought much on it that way."

Jim stood up, walked over to the wood box, talking all the time, eyes deliberately avoiding Mike's. "Man ought to take politickin' with a grain of salt. Politicians got ways of twistin' words."

"Seems plain enough to me," Mike said bluntly. "And any white man who's fathered nigger brats ought to be run out of the country."

Jim took a couple of sticks of firewood over to the stove, shoved them into the glowing coals, set the coffeepot back on the eye. He looked out at Mike, explained honestly, "Most men come west leavin' a past they'd just as soon forget. Out here a man looks to the future."

Mike stood up, headed toward the door. "It's true, then?"

Jim followed, talking. "Mike, you got to remember that was a long time ago. In another world, a white man's world. Made by him, controlled by him. You can't condemn a man in this world for what he done in that world."

Mike stayed silent, still surly.

The screen door at the ranch house slammed shut. Frank Driskill stepped out on the porch. At the sight of the two men approaching, Frank said, "Jim, them horses get over to that wagon train?"

"Yeah. Ramon seen to it."

"Fine. Let's go see if they moved on."

Mike had a hangdog look about him, eyes studying the ground. He spoke into space, even as he started to his horse. "I don't feel up to it. . . . Think I'll join the boys out on the south range."

"Thought you might ride over to them wagons with us, see how them folks made out," Frank said hopefully.

"I ain't much up to it, Pa," Mike said gloomily, and mounted up. "Besides that," he said from the saddle, "no use in all three of us wastin' time over there with them nig-gers. They likely made out all right, since you gave them MFD stock,'' Mike added sarcastically, swinging his sorrel roughly and cantering away.

Frank just stood there, watching Mike go. He couldn't believe what he had just heard. Then, turning to Jim, he asked, ''What ails him?

''He's been porin' over that newspaper that come in yes-terday. That story about white men stickin' up for coloreds got to him. Takin' it hard.''

''Read that tripe myself,'' Frank said bitterly. ''This takes the cake, Jim! Them Democrats are stirrin' in a nasty pile now. A lot of men don't take to this kind of talk. Not even some Democrats. It's somethin' we all ought to let die nat-urally.''

They had started to their horses. After they mounted up, Jim said, ''Them was mostly my exact words to Mike.''

Frank Driskill swung his horse away sharply, took out at a fast gallop. Jim Seely spurred out, trying to catch up.

For womenfolk ranch life was lonely, isolated. Most big ranchmen quartered their women and children in a town house in the nearest settlement to be near social activity and schooling, if they had youngsters. The women visited the ranch frequently, and ranchmen would stay in town from time to time. It was a working arrangement that suited most womenfolk and working ranchmen.

Thirty-five miles northeast at Santa Angela, Nora Driskill sat at the breakfast table, her graying head buried in the newspaper, the *Santa Angela Bee*. Deep furrows of worry had just now popped up, joining the shallow crow's-foot lines of age. The second cup of coffee the Mexican maid had sat before her was lukewarm now. Nora hadn't sipped in a good while. She was absorbed in the brazen insinuations of editor Sal McMahan.

Nora lifted her dark blue eyes and with trembling fingers pushed back a thin wisp of graying hair that had fallen at her temple, staring deeply off into emptiness, her mind reaching back. Suddenly, as if prompted by some unseen voice, she summoned her maid: "Conchita!"

Conchita popped her head around the kitchen doorjamb, eyebrows lifting, asked a question, "*Sí,* senora?"

"Tell Pico I'll want to go out to the ranch tomorrow," Nora said calmly. "We'll take the usual provisions. Leave at the usual time."

"Senora, is something wrong?"

"No. Of course not."

Chapter Ten

The ferry floated Cole briskly down and across Nueces River, a wide ribbon of muddy water rippling on the surface, roiling on downstream.

At the other shoreline, he pulled the ropes, hauled the flatbed raft into the landing dock. He led the bay ashore, scouted the immediate vicinity.

Sign showed the horse herd had indeed been ferried across. Chopped-up sand, fresh dung, the odd-shaped shoeprints of the Andalusians clearly present. The trail led south. Cole lifted his eyes there.

Nothing. A vast nothingness of shimmering heatwaves. Even the sun seemingly hung out there motionless, throwing out a brassy circle of punishing heat.

He drew the back of a sweaty palm across his forehead, wiped away sweat and trail dust, his mind thinking over the danger of riding into that vast cauldron out there. Even now, off in the distance he could see a parched, shriveled hide clinging to the ribs of a rotting horse. And just to the left of

119

that the hulk of a broken half-buried wagon, a wheel's wooden spokes pointing warning fingers of death to the sky.

What Cole was looking out across was that bone-dry, scorching-hot stretch of wasteland between the Nueces and Rio Grande Rivers. It was wasteland on the southern fringe of that fiery hell upchucked by ancient volcano eruptions long ago and named by early Spaniards the Despoblado, or uninhabited land. The only things that survived out here had horns, thorns, or rattlers. And needed precious little water. Apaches qualified on the last count.

Apaches travel light in small bands, and can easily go two, three days without water. More if traveling alone, which they do often.

So why were Rudolpho and the others driving a dozen prime horses out here?

If a man wanted to sell or trade good riding stock there was no better place than across the Rio Grande. Many a man made a living wage at it, too. But a man had to know what for. Even a tenderfoot could see this was a hellacious place to cross into Mexico. And Rudolpho was nobody's tenderfoot.

So why would they do it?

Cole mounted up, touched spurs to the bay, following the tracks. He had no choice. He'd been trusted to bring the horses.

Where he rode was table-flat, rust-colored land scattered with forests of prickly pear, sotol bushes, agaritas, and bunches of sacahuiste grass.

Thirty minutes later by the sun he pulled to a halt, twisted around in the saddle, checking his backtrail.

Nothing moved back there. Even the thorny whiplike branches of the tasajillo he had passed hung limp in the hot air.

Cole dismounted, led the bay out of the chopped-up trail carved up by the horse herd moving ahead of him. Fifty yards off to the side he tied his horse to a bush. With gloved hand he ripped up sacahuiste grass, made a nice bundle, a broom. Careful to backtrack in his own steps, he returned to the trail of the horse herd. He carefully swept out his own tracks and the dun's. It wasn't a professional job, but it would take a watchful eye to notice that a lone rider had left the trail.

And that's what he did. He mounted up and rode north at a canter.

It just didn't figure. Rudolpho heading for the Rio Grande this way. Cole had a hunch. And he would play it.

Seven hard-riding, trail-dusted men ran their heavily lathered horses up to Arnolds Crossing on the Nueces River. The leader pulled to a hard stop, the others following suit, kicking up a cloud of dust that trailed on out over the running water.

The leader was a lanky hawk-nosed man, thirty-something. Name of Harley Sweat. Harley was a rawboned, lanternjawed man. He was range-hardened by sun and wind, toughened by hard, steady work.

Harley was the foreman for Morgan Hamilton, and was a hard-driven man. He had narrow goals, no inkling whatever of failing. Whatever it was that Morgan Hamilton ordered, Harley did. And just now his hard, experienced eyes were focused across the river to where the ferry was tied up where Cole had left it.

What Harley saw, he didn't like.

Harley swore under his breath. He turned in the saddle, ran his eyes around the buildings. Then he brought his horse around, gigged him toward Chancey's Saloon.

Kelly, Will, and Juan were still sitting at the table in the far-off corner talking when seven hot, thirsty men filed into the saloon and scattered along the bar. Three pairs of eyes followed the procession inquisitively, but three pairs of lips kept shut.

Harley looked to be the leader, and the walrus-mustached bartender took him as such. "Drinks, senor?" he asked Harley.

"Beer all round," Harley said, shucking a work glove. While the bartender was drawing the beers, Harley asked, "Ferry seen any use lately?"

"*Sí*, senor. All the time."

"Say in the last hour or so?"

The bartender slid one mug of beer down the bar. "*Sí*, senor. That too," and he shoved down another beer, slyly cutting his eyes over at Kelly.

Harley caught the eye movement. He had been standing slack-legged; now he drew up alertly, suspicious of something.

The bartender shoved down two more beers, walked down with the last ones in his hands.

Harley picked up his beer with his left hand, and with his right hand snaked his gun from its holster, laid it on the bar, the barrel pointing ten inches below the bartender's chest. "Want some straight answers," he said bluntly. "Give 'em and you got no trouble."

The bartender's eyes widened, his voice caught. "S-*sí*, senor. No trouble."

"You lookin' for information, mister?" a voice from over in the corner asked.

Harley straightened and turned around, faced the voice. His eyes met a man with a bloodstained bandanna wrapped around his gun hand, obviously a fresh wound. "Yeah, I'm lookin' for information," Harley said, and leaned back, rested his elbows on the bar, his gun hand free. "No more'n an hour ago some horses come through here, all blooded stock."

"Saaay, that's right," Kelly said mockingly. "Seems you know the answers already."

"They cross the ferry?" Harley asked seriously.

"Like clockwork."

"Six . . . seven men?"

"Six. One of them a big fancy-dressed Mes'can hombre. Overheard talk they was headin' for the Rio Grande." Kelly smiled knowingly.

"You don't believe it?" Harley asked.

Kelly chuckled lightly. "A man would have to be a plumb fool to try it the way they was headed. And that Mex didn't look the fool to me."

"If a man had to guess, where would you say them horses are likely to wind up?"

"I'd guess they'll swim them horses back across the river tonight."

Will, sitting at the table next to Kelly, leaned forward on his elbows, said teasingly, " 'Course, that other feller that rode in here behind them might have somethin' to say about that. He seemed right capable."

"Seen tracks of a lone rider trailin' after them," Harley said. "Never laid eyes on him, though. What's he look like?"

Kelly shrugged, spread his hands apart carelessly. "You seen one nigger, you seen 'em all."

"He was a little better'n six feet tall, I'd guess," Will said. "Light-complected. In his early twenties. Had on some of them big Mexican chaps and was ridin' a blood bay horse."

"He the one give you that?" Harley asked, nodding and dropping his eyes down to Kelly's smashed-up gun hand.

"None of your damn business!" Kelly snapped.

"Senor, he is quick . . . very quick," Juan interrupted.

"Black man?" Harley asked.

"*Sí*."

Harley chuckled. "Hell, I never seen one yet that was." Harley faced back around to the bar, tossed off his drink. "Drink up, boys. We got business to see after."

Seven men walked away from the bar, spurs jingling.

Juan said a last word aloud at Harley's back: "Senor, this one, he is dangerous. *Puro hombre* . . . all man."

Harley paid him no mind. What the Mexican had just said was scare talk, just scare talk!

At the flank of a shallow sandhill concealed by a cluster of prickly pears, Cole sat his horse in the shadows, taking in the sights and sounds of Rancho Los Ojuelos. Across the waist-high adobe wall he could see heads of Mexican women moving around in the plaza, shoulders of burros browsing. Mighty little activity as far as menfolk went. Only one man. A sentry in the church belfry.

Cole nudged his horse forward, swung into the wagon road leading to the portals. And right away his hunch paid off: the tracks of the big Andalusians. Other hoofprints too. Earth chewed up badly, recently.

The horses were here, all right. And Cole meant to have them. Rudolpho be damned!

He walked the bay under the portals, entered the plaza.

It was hot. Perspiration pocked his face, darkened his armpits. He dismounted next to six sweat-stained ponies standing head down in front of the cantina. Knocking the thong off his pistol, he looked around, sizing up the place.

A flea-bitten dog was lying in the shade of some morning glories growing along the adobe wall. A gamecock was scratching away at the hard-packed earth. The sentry in the lookout tower was standing at the rail, rifle held at the ready in his two hands. A Mexican woman stopped washing to watch him.

He stepped across the threshold, walked inside the cantina,

a low-roofed, dirt-floored affair. A rectangle of sunlight streamed in through the opening at his back.

Six tough-looking men were lined up at the bar, their wide sombreros looking like a garden of giant mushrooms.

Cole's spurs had jingled.

The man closest turned, looked that way. His eyes flared at the sight of Cole. Elbowing the Mexican next to him, he said excitedly, "Compadre, it is him!"

The big wide-chested man next to him deliberately placed his tequila glass down on the bar, turned around slowly. Rudolpho!

Cole was standing just inside the door, facing Rudolpho.

Rudolpho smiled wide, but his eyes were hard, steady. "It is you again, amigo?" His voice was pleasant but had a deadly ring to it. "Did you bring the dead again, my friend?"

"No," Cole said mildly, "but the dead have a way of turning up."

Rudolpho smiled quickly. "Senor, you chase the horse thieves one way, then you chase the horse thieves another way. My friend, make up your mind." Careful not to make a sudden move, Rudolpho deliberately brought his hand to his chin, loosened the rawhide chin strap on his sombrero.

"My mind's already made up," Cole said, even as Rudolpho's hand started up.

"And what is your mind?" Rudolpho took hold of the brim of his sombrero, casually lifted it clear of his head.

"My mind tells me my horses are here," Cole answered.

Rudolpho smiled innocently. The sombrero started to come down.

Cole shot him. Then shot into his body again.

Rudolpho's fingers had released the sombrero and had darted for his gun. That sombrero was a trick Cole knew about. Cole's pistol had come level, spit, then spit again. Rudolpho was knocked back, the bullet slamming into his chest.

His eyes went wide with shock, the smile frozen in place on his lips.

Rudolpho got his pistol out just as the sombrero hit the floor. His gun came up. And that's when Cole fired into him again.

What Rudolpho had tried was an old gunfighter's trick brought in from Sonora. The moment that sombrero swept down innocently, concealing the hand, the sombrero is dropped, the hand darting for the gun. To the unsuspecting man, it was deadly, like giving the other man a head start on the draw.

There were still five of them standing there at the bar. But Cole's six-shooter was aimed right where it could do some harm. None of them doubted someone among them would die before they got Cole. And from the way they were looking at each other, not one of them was willing to chance it.

"I got business with Don Jose," Cole said. "Not with none of you."

The Mexican on the end shot a sideward glance at the one standing next to him. These were proud men. They rode for Don Jose. None of them would willingly stand by idly and see the Don shot to death.

"Only talkin' business," Cole said reassuringly. "Don Jose is a good man. He will listen, no?" Before anybody could answer, he indicated the walrus-mustached Mexican standing rigidly behind the bar. "You! Come over here!" He took the Mexican by the scruff of the collar, guided him to the door space. Looking up at the man in the tower, Cole said, "Tell him I go to see Don Jose." He cocked his pistol at the man's ear. "Tell him to throw the rifle down!"

The Mexican shouted something in his own tongue. Presently a rifle sailed through the air, clattered down onto the hard-packed earth below. Sidestepping out the open space, his gun leveled back inside, Cole said, "*Adiós,* amigos."

Following closely the adobe wall of the cantina, he took

wary steps, making his way toward the hacienda down at the end of the plaza where Don Jose lived.

"Senor, there is no need," said an amused voice from across the street. "You are still welcome here."

Don Jose. Dona Maria at his side. Coming out of the church across the street. Don Jose had heard shots from the cantina and was coming to investigate.

Cole stopped. Seeing who it was, he holstered his gun, came away from the adobe wall, walking across the plaza to meet Don Jose, saying as he came, "Your *caporal* didn't think I was still welcome."

"Rudolpho? He is a good man, a proud man, amigo."

"And a horse thief."

Jose smiled thinly. "Senor, do not take it unkindly. It is the way of things here."

"The way of a hangin'."

Suddenly an excited voice rang down from the tower. "Don Jose! Men come!" And the guard pointed toward the river.

"How many?" Don Jose asked up at him.

"*Siete* . . . seven."

"Morgan Hamilton's men," Cole said. "They followed me. Coming after horses too."

"I think so too, amigo," Jose replied. "But there are means." Jose ordered Dona Maria, "To the hacienda! There will be shooting." After a firm shove, Maria ran on her way, looking back anxiously a time or two.

Then Jose shouted to the women and children in the plaza, "Senoritas! Muchachos! Trouble comes! Vamoose!"

The Mexicans inside the cantina ran outside into the plaza. Don Jose said to the tall one, "Morales, gringos come! To your positions!"

Cole ran over, scooped up the rifle the sentry had tossed over the side earlier. "Senor, you will need this," Cole said, calling up to him, and tossed the rifle up barrel first. The

Mexican caught it out of the air. "*Gracias,* amigo."

Don Jose looked questioningly at Cole. "You will join our fight?"

"I got two horses in that bunch."

"Then we will teach the gringos a lesson," Jose said. Running over to one of the horses standing in front of the cantina, he yanked a Winchester from the saddle scabbard. "To the portals!" he yelled to Cole, sweeping his hand.

Chapter Eleven

Fifty yards from the portals of Rancho Los Ojuelos, Harley sat his saddle, studying the layout, a half-dozen riders in a loose knot fanned out at his back.

Harley didn't like what he saw. The rancho was armed, ready: Two men stood waiting at the portals with Winchesters. He could see at least two rifle barrels peeking over the adobe walls from each corner. Men were up in the belfry.

Harley wiped sweat from his brow. This time things were different. Twice before he had retrieved stolen horses from this rancho, once while the horses had been out on the graze range, and once under cover of darkness he and his men had driven horses from a pole corral in the canyon that ran in back of the hacienda. Harley could see that this time the only way he was going to retrieve horses from the canyon was by a shooting fight.

And the men riding with him knew it too. A lanky cowpuncher next to Harley raked his tongue nervously over dry lips and spoke. "Them horses ain't goin' nowheres, Harley. Let's let them be for now."

"We'll talk," Harley said out the side of his mouth. "Fight if we have to." Harley nudged his horse forward.

A dozen or so yards from the portals, Don Jose's voice reached out to Harley. "Senor, you have business?"

Harley pulled up easily. "Lookin' for stolen horses . . . blooded stock." Harley saw Cole for the first time. "Wearing Box H brand."

"It is a brand known well," Don Jose replied. "Such a mistake could not be made, amigo."

"Unless somebody intended to do some brand-blottin'," Harley said, shifting in his saddle. "Or run them across the river."

Jose smiled slightly. "Senor, that is unthinkable." Without warning Jose's pretentiousness vanished. "Enough idle talk! What is your business?"

"All right!" Harley snapped. "Here it is. Your vaqueros drove off Box H stock. Tracks show them horses were run in here." Harley leaned forward in his saddle, stacked his two hands on the pommel, made his voice a direct accusation. "Them horses are held in the canyon back yonder." Harley nodded that way.

"*Sí*, they are there," Jose said agreeably. "Senor Hamilton has been warned. His law is meaningless here. . . ."

Suddenly a fusillade of rifle fire erupted from down the canyon.

The guard in the tower yelled, "Don Jose! The horses!" Just at that moment the ugly *whump* of a bullet dug into his chest, knocking him over the guardrail, sprawling him out in the plaza below.

Harley was standing in his stirrups, straining his eyes at the cloud of dust surging toward them from down the canyon. "Indians!" Harley screamed. "Take cover!" Harley jumped out of the saddle with his Winchester in his land, landed on a dead run, heading for cover behind the adobe wall.

Shug Tilson was mounted next to Harley. As soon as he started to leave the saddle a bullet broke into his skull. He was dead before his other toe left the stirrup. His horse trotted the body into the plaza.

The roiling cloud of dust kicked up by running horses was no more than thirty yards off, directly in front of the portals now. Bullets thudded against the adobe wall, zinged through the air all around Harley and his men crouched down behind the adobe wall. Rolly Jimson, a short bull of a man with a long blue bandanna around his neck, had already taken a bullet in the thigh vaulting the wall.

Cole and Don Jose each had a rifle steadied on top of the wall, looking along the barrel, searching the cloud of dust for a target.

The two Mexicans who had run up in the tower were the only ones who could see above the drifting dust and were firing at will. An Indian pitched forward, slumped over his horse's mane, holding on precariously.

Suddenly it was over. In less than a minute.

Two men lay dead, another wounded, the horses gone.

Harley ran out under the portals, swore bitterly, then shot his rifle in rapid-fire succession at the solid blanket of trail dust going away from him.

Don Jose came out from behind cover, brushing dust from his waistcoat. "Senor," he said pleasantly to Harley, "Morgan Hamilton's horses." And Jose nodded his head after the fleeing horses. "They are yours if you wish."

Harley eyed Jose coldly, his jaw rigid.

"My horses too," Cole said, stepping away from the wall, Winchester held carelessly along his leg.

"You will go after your horses, senor?" Jose asked, surprised.

Cole walked on toward his horse, talking all the time.

"Man sent me to fetch horses. I aim to." And he kept on walking.

Jose exchanged glances with Harley.

At his horse, Cole shoved his Winchester into the saddle scabbard, stepped a toe into the stirrup, swung into the leather. Turning his horse, he cantered over to the church, asked up at the man in the tower, "How many you figure?"

The man wagged his head negatively and shrugged. The other man in the tower, an older man, came over to the rail, holding a palm over his right biceps, a trickle of red visible. Obviously a flesh would. *"Ocho . . . nueve,"* he said.

"Eight . . . nine," Don Jose translated.

Cole swung the bay, walked him toward the portals.

"I'm damned if he ain't fool enough to go out there alone," Harley said, looking perplexed at Jose.

Under the portals Cole went, running his horse, heading after the trail dust.

"He's crazy! Plumb crazy!" said Rolly.

"Maybe not," Harley said flatly, studying the ground.

"You ain't thinkin' of goin' out there?" Rolly asked.

"Mr. Hamilton would be mighty put out to lose them horses," Harley said seriously. "And I ain't lookin' forward to tellin' him we lost them. Rolly, you boys take Shug's body on back to the ranch. Tell Mr. Hamilton the story." Harley retrieved his horse, which had trotted into the plaza. He mounted up, walked his horse out to the portals, stopped. He faced around and said to Rolly, "I'll be back in a day or so. Might be the both of us," and he nodded out toward where Cole had headed, "can surprise them Indians, get the horses back."

Rolly, standing there on his gimpy leg, spit on the ground. "Indians don't surprise worth a damn, boss. You know that."

"Expect they won't," Harley agreed grimly. "See that Mr. Hamilton gets the full story. He'll know what to do."

"Okay, boss."

Harley slapped spurs to his horse, took out after Cole's trail dust.

The Overland Stage Line had a daily mail route from San Antonio to Tubac. The road was safe because it ran too close to settlements for troublesome Indians and was too much out in the open for highwaymen. It was a well-used road, good and level. So the stage was always on time. Each day a passenger or two accompanied the mail.

Today was no different. At exactly high noon the heavy-voiced driver Arnold "Sixshooter" Boyd barked a "Whoaaa" to the team and hauled the Concord coach to a stop in front of the post office that served as the stage stop. The man riding the box fussed around with mail and baggage. Sixshooter swung down, opened the passenger door. "Tubac, folks," he announced.

Sixshooter peeled back the sand-colored duster he was wearing, withdrew a gold watch from his shirt pocket, announced inside the coach, "You folks goin' on up the line welcome to stretch yo'selfs for ten minutes. Then we move out."

A small middle-aged man stepped down out of the coach, looking around. Sixshooter said to him respectfully, "Hope you had a pleasant journey, Mr. Matthews."

"That I did, Sixshooter . . . that I did," Olny Matthews said, stepping aside.

A tall thin man stepped down from the coach next. He faced around, looked up and down the boardwalk. Annoyed at the almost primitive conditions, he turned up his nose, brushed dirt from the gray suit he had on, obviously disappointed. There was irritation in his voice when he spoke. "Mr. Matthews," he said stiffily, "I've no desire to remain in this town any longer than necessary. Shall we be about our business?"

"Of course, Mr. Biggers."

Olny Matthews and Zell Biggers politely walked away from the coach, heading down the street to the Exchange Hotel.

Sixshooter had taken in the whole thing. Now he tipped back his battered hat, said derisively behind their backs in a low voice, "A pleasure haulin' y'alls asses, sir."

On the second floor of the Exchange Hotel in a room that fronted the street, Morgan Hamilton's eyes glowed with pleasure at the sight of Olny and Zell. Sitting there behind his desk, he leaned back in his comfortable chair, smiled broadly, said, "Zell, I never expected to see the likes of you in Tubac. What brings you?"

"Senator's orders," Zell replied dryly. "He's worried, Morgan. You've got to play this right."

"Why, sure, Zell," Morgan said reassuringly. "Nothing for Senator Mullis to worry over. This'll be a snap. The pieces are all fallin' into place."

Morgan turned his attention to Olny. "Did you get what you went after?"

"More than I expected. That editor over at San Antonio I told you about . . . Sal McMahan, he had names, all right. I got the one you're interested in. Took some talkin', though."

"And cash on the barrelhead," Zell added.

"Good . . . good," Morgan beamed.

"And Zell here has somethin' the senator thinks you ought to see."

From his gripsack Zell produced a book the size of a mail-order catalogue. He slid the book across the desktop in front of Morgan's eyes. Morgan drew back, startled. "What's this?" he asked.

"That's what you wanted," Zell said. "Frank Driskill's past. It's all in there."

Morgan exchanged looks with Olny.

Olny nodded. "It's there, all right. That book there . . . it's called the Outlaw Book. Only five men in the state know that book exists. Four captains of Rangers, and the governor hisself. Word is, one of the captains, Captain McNelly, put that book together. That's where Sal got his information for the editorial."

The corners of Morgan's mouth stretched into a smile. He picked up the book, riffled the pages. Lifting his eyebrows at Zell, he asked, "Senator Mullis?"

"That's right. But if things blow up Senator Mullis knows nothing. Not a darn thing. As far as he's concerned, Tubac is dead. Without the railroad, and all."

"Maybe not," replied Morgan pensively. "If a man was to play his cards right, there's pickings to be had."

"And you figure to do the picking?"

"Why not? With the coloreds disarmed only one man stands in my way. And if there's evidence in this book to back up what that editor said, I'm holding the ace in the hole." Morgan tapped the Outlaw Book.

"There's evidence there," Zell answered. "But be warned, Morgan. If your scheme sours, you forget you know Senator Mullis. Them's his words exactly."

Morgan shoved back his chair, stood up behind his desk. "Zell, give the senator my regards," he said dismissively. "Tell the desk clerk Mr. Hamilton said to fix you up with a comfortable room till the next stage leaves for San Antonio. I'll see the bill is paid."

Zell Biggers took up his gripsack. He and Olny had started for the door when next Morgan spoke again: "Oh, Olny . . . I'll need a word with you."

Zell Biggers quietly closed the door behind him.

Morgan came from behind his desk, rested a palm on Olny's shoulder. "Olny, that was a first-rate job you did. I like that in a man."

"My pleasure, Mr. Hamilton."

"A man in my position can't have too many of the right kinds of friends. I won't forget you, Olny." Guiding him by the shoulder, Morgan started Olny toward the door. "Oh, Olny, you see Marshal Ashbel on the street, send him up, will you?"

"Sure thing, Mr. Hamilton."

A long time after Olny had gone, Morgan was still sitting behind his desk gloating over what the Outlaw Book had to say about Frank Driskill's past.

Somebody rapped on the door.

The rapping scarcely broke his concentration. He responded absentmindedly, "Come in."

Marshal Ashbel opened the door, walked across the threshold. "You wanted to see me?"

Morgan did not lift his eyes from the page as he ordered, "Sit down over there, Ashbel." He pointed indifferently. "I'll be with you in a minute."

Two minutes later Morgan flapped the book shut, satisfied. He lifted his eyes to Ashbel. "Things are beginning to fall into place, Ashbel," he said, beaming. "How are the boys?"

"No trouble, Mr. Hamilton. They just sittin' and waitin' for your orders."

"Good. Take a couple of the boys, ride over to Santa Angela. Now, here's what I want you to do. . . ."

Three men walked their horses down Santa Angela's main street. They had come a long way in a hurry, their horses gaunt, played out. The thin man with the rawhide vest on rode slump-shouldered, dead tired. All three men had stubble on their faces, clothes dirty from the trail.

They turned their horses to the hitch rail in front of the sign that said SHERIFF, pulled to a halt, dismounted wearily.

The man with the vest on eyed two loafers sitting on the bench there, asked politely, "Sheriff in?"

"He's in," said the man sitting on the end of the bench, nodding his head inside.

Boot heels clumping across the boardwalk, the three men filed into the sheriff's office.

Sheriff Ralph Tucker was leaning back in an armchair behind his desk, palms clasped behind his head, daydreaming, his booted feet propped up on the desk. At the unexpected sight of the three men the sheriff dropped his feet to the floor, came upright, his eyes asking a question.

"Sheriff Tucker?" asked the vested man.

"That's right."

"I'm Marshal Ashbel from over at Tubac." Ashbel drew back the flap of his rawhide vest, revealing his badge. "This here's Mort and Burt," he said, nodding.

"Seems I've heard the name," said Tucker. "This business or what?"

Ashbel looked down his nose disrespectfully at Tucker. "I take it you heard of Morgan Hamilton, ain't you?" Ashbel asked.

"Mr. Hamilton?" Tucker repeated, lifting his eyebrows. "Why, sure! Who hasn't?"

"You can drop the playacting," Ashbel said.

Tucker got attentive.

"Mr. Hamilton needs a job done," Ashbel said. "And you're to see that it gets done."

"What's that mean?" Tucker asked innocently.

Ashbel reached into his vest pocket, came out with a newspaper clipping, tossed it on Tucker's desk. "Read that first . . . and I'll fill in details."

The newspaper article that Tucker stared at was the malicious editorial written by Sal McMahan. At the top of the article was handwritten "Frank Driskill."

Tucker read the article slowly, lifted gleaming eyes to Ashbel, then read it again. "I always thought so all along," he said proudly. "Things was always just too cozy between Frank and that boy."

"Now you know it for sure," Ashbel said. "And you're to see that every white man in town knows it."

Tucker's mind thought ahead. He thought of the kind of man Frank Driskill was. And he could see the danger he was being led into. He knew Frank would kill him. "Now lookahere," he said, flustered. "Anybody spread word like that around . . . Driskill wouldn't stand still for it. There'd be killin' for sure."

"You're the sheriff, ain't you? Besides that, that's why we're here . . . to back up your play."

"Well, yeah . . . but—"

"The way I figure it," Ashbel interrupted, "all a man would have to do is drop a few loose words across the street," and he indicated the Bon Ton Saloon. "Saloon talk naturally spreads. . . ." Ashbel smiled knowingly. "You got some boys sittin' round on their duffs out front who ought to be good at that sort of thing. Who's to say who started it?"

"Yeah, who's to say," Tucker said, brightening.

Ashbel eyed Tucker coolly, then, starting out the door, said back, "We'll stick around till the ball gets rollin'. Wouldn't want to ride back and give Mr. Hamilton the wrong impression."

Marshal Ashbel, Mort Stall, and Burt Lindley had mounted their horses when Sheriff Tucker came out on the boardwalk. They wheeled their mounts, rode off. They didn't hear Sheriff Tucker tell the slack-jawed man sitting there, "I've got a job for you and the boys." Tucker came out of his pocket with a fold of bills, peeled off one from the top, passed it over. "You boys go over to the Bon Ton, get yourselves something to drink. Drop word that. . . ."

*　　*　　*

High Prairie

Hours later a man clip-clopped his horse up to the hitchrail in front of the Bon Ton. He sat in the saddle for a long minute, contemplating, then he swung down. He was tall. Thick-muscled. A youngster.

It was Mike Driskill. His solid jaws were set tight, his face holding a grim look of things gone wrong. Impulsively he whipped his reins into a careless half-hitch around the hitchrail, then stomped away, heading toward the Bon Ton Saloon. Mike was mad. It showed. And he had reason to be.

Slightly less than an hour before, he had been sitting at the breakfast table across from his mother. The article he had read and the tiff with his father had driven him into town. Considering their past, he knew that, like himself, his mother would worry over the insinuations of the article.

So Mike had left the range, rode into town to console his mother . . . and to seek consolation for his own thoughts.

Nora Driskill was a tough-minded woman who had endured the harsh realities of a past life of slave owning. Her parting words to Mike had been "Your pa and me promised to bury the past when we come out here. You go on back to the ranch. Your pa needs you now."

Mike had left there troubled, confused. His first impulse had been to lash out at someone, anyone. His next impulse had been to have a drink, think things through.

Now he was here. His two hands rested on top of the batwing doors of the Bon Ton Saloon, poised to push through.

He pushed through, crossed over the threshold, looking around.

The place grew quiet when they saw who it was. The music stopped. Even the bartender seemed not to look up at him.

Did they suspect? Could they know?

"Beer," Mike said to the bartender, tossing a coin on the bar.

Out of the corner of his eye Mike caught sight of a thick, slack-jawed man leaning over, talking close to the ear of the man sitting across from him, obviously saying something he didn't want Mike to hear. Somebody over at the next table chuckled lightly. And then a man next to him tugged the brim of his hat down over his face, as if he was ashamed for Mike to look at him.

The bartender slid the beer down rudely in front of Mike, left the coin where it lay.

"What's the latest talk, Wally?" Mike asked lightheartedly.

"Usual range talk," the bartender answered, and moved down the bar.

Mike picked up his drink, tossed off half of it, set the mug down. Facing around, he ran his eyes over the room, looking for somebody friendly.

Three strangers were sitting at the table in the far corner. One wore a rawhide vest. Three of Sheriff Tucker's flunkies occupied the table next to them. Mike recognized the tall loose-jawed one, Ned Potter.

A hawk-faced man with a carpet of white hair covering his face was at a table next to the wall. Sitting next to him was a leathery-faced Mexican, looked to be a sheepherder. There were at least six or seven other cowhands seated throughout the place killing time.

Nobody said anything.

But their faces were awfully smug, Mike thought.

And he could just hear them talking behind his back before he came in.

A pushed-back chair scraped across the floor. The man next to Potter stood up, hitched up his low-slung gun belt. He stared long and hard at Mike, a scornful look. Then he said in an ugly voice, "You ain't welcome in here. None of you Driskills are."

Mike was already in a foul mood. The man's biting words

brought back the nasty taste in his mouth he had been trying to get rid of.

Mike faced him directly. "I don't know you, mister, but if you got something to say, say it plain."

"Name's Ike . . . Ike Booker. I'll say it plain. No use in you Driskills tryin' to live a lie around here no more. Word is around. Your pa got a nigger kid. You got a nigger brother. We don't want your kind 'round here."

Mike's face turned two shades whiter, then flushed crimson. The bottom of his stomach felt as if it wanted to drop out. He fought back the urge to smash something, anything.

It took a good ten seconds for him to compose himself. "That's a lie!" he screamed. Then he announced, "And any man who repeats it better fill his hands!" He roved his eyes over the tight-lipped men staring out at him, seeing if there were any takers.

Nobody said anything. The place was eerily quiet; the bartender had conveniently disappeared. Out front a horse blew, shook.

Suddenly it dawned on Mike. This was all a setup. He was being baited into a gunfight. He shifted his eyes to the stranger wearing the vest. "This your idea?"

Ashbel smiled thinly, shrugged his shoulders. "You called the man a liar. Any fool kid knows what that means."

Somebody over at the next table snickered softly.

Now Mike knew.

The thing was, Mike was quick with a gun, very quick. He and Cole had practiced against each other ever since Mike had been allowed to wear his own pistol at the age of fourteen. Cole already had one. When he was only seventeen Mike could have notched his pistol twice if he had wanted to. More than that if you counted Indians.

Mike spread his feet apart, relaxed his gun hand down to his side, eyes watching Ike Booker like a hawk.

"Your pa—"

Mike started shooting. Ike never got another word out.

Marshal Ashbel took the first bullet in the center of his chest, knocking him over backward, chair and all. Ashbel was sitting at the table next to where Ike was standing. He had had his gun hand out of sight under the table. The slight lean of his right shoulder had warned Mike that the hand was holding a gun under the table. Mike knew that if he was to have any chance at all, he had to get that man first. And that's where his first shot went. Ashbel's gun never fired. It dropped to the floor under the table. His body crumpled away from the chair, spread-eagled out onto the floor, arms flung wide, vest front open.

When Mike fired that first shot, he ducked to his right. And that's what saved him.

Ike's pistol exploded just as Mike squeezed off his next shot. The bullets had to have crossed each other in flight, because both men went reeling at exactly the same instant.

Ike's bullet tore at Mike's shirt on the left side, scorching a nasty furrow along the skin from front to back.

Ike wasn't so lucky. Mike's bullet broke into his chest at the top of his breastbone, exploded up, tearing at his throat. Somehow Ike wasn't dead instantly. His bloody mouth tried to say something. But nothing came out. Just gurgling sounds. Then he was gone.

Mort and Burt were completely stunned by the way things had turned out. They both had been cocksure the trap had been neatly set, Mike a dead man. Now they were at a loss over what to do. Make a play or get up and walk out. They both knew one thing for sure: The kid's pistol was a single-action Navy Colt. Repeater, six shots. And he was fast with it, very fast . . . and accurate.

Instinctively Mike ran his fingers over the wet spot where the pain was coming from. Blood. Roving his eyes over the room, he said harshly, "It was a lie! And any man who repeats it is a liar."

Ned Potter smiled, a crooked, deceitful smile, and said accusingly, "Driskill, you just shot a lawman."

"He didn't act like no lawman," Mike replied flatly.

"Badge is plain as day."

Mike kept his eyes on Ned, but out of the corner of his eye he could see a badge shining where Ashbel's vest had fallen open.

The hawk-faced man with the snow-white beard spoke up. "Driskill, you were lucky that time. You ought to clear out of here while you can."

"Its a lie!" Mike snarled. "And I'll kill any man who repeats it!" he added, backstepping toward the batwings. Twice he stumbled on the way to his horse. Struggling onto the saddle, he gathered up the reins, trotted his horse out. After no more than a minute's canter pain shot across his side, dizziness started to creep over him. A mile out of town he wrapped the reins around the saddle horn, gave the horse his head, heading toward the MFD.

Chapter Twelve

Cole was riding hard, following in the tracks of the horse herd driven by the Indians. The canyon mouth had gradually flared out into a wide funnel. Now it was a broad plain of scrub mesquite and cholla cactus. Up ahead he could see undulating wild grass, stretching away as far as his eyes could see. The high plains.

He twisted around in the saddle, checked his backtrail again. A knowing man will do that from time to time, riding wild country. A look back, even if not for enemies, gives a man a different perspective on the land, a different view of landmarks and such.

Again Cole looked back. Quickly looked back again. There was trail dust being thrown up back there! He checked the bay down to a shambling trot, twisted around in the saddle, double-checking.

That was trail dust, all right. A thin ribbon of brown against the horizon.

He lashed his horse, raising him into a gallop. He raced

out of the middle of the canyon, angling over to the right side. Near the canyon wall he reined in in a forest of prickly pears and waited, eyes searching his backtrail, trying to identify who it was following him.

Harley! The man called Harley back there at Los Ojuelos.

Cole could see that Harley was riding his saddle expertly, moving perfectly in rhythm with the horse's motion, his hat brim turned up by the wind, the big chestnut eating up distance in a smooth gallop.

Harley rode with his eyes scouting the chopped-up earth in front of him.

Where the bay's tracks veered off to the right, leading off to the canyon wall, Harley pounded leather on down the middle of the canyon floor, following the horse herd.

Right away Cole had recognized the tall, thin-chested man as Harley. But why was he out here? The Indians had Morgan Hamilton's horses, true enough. But Hamilton was a man of means, Cole had heard, and could get any horse he wanted with ease.

Cole knew that one rider dogging the Indian's trail was a dangerous, chancy thing in itself. But two men? He had his doubts.

Apaches were patient, thorough. Born with the instincts and cunning of a she-coon. Keen-eyed. Watchful. They could spot a man's trail dust a mile away.

Cole made up his mind right there. He didn't want Harley coming along. He wanted no part of Harley's company.

He stopped his horse, sat in the saddle, watching Harley pounding leather, then saw him disappear around the curve in the canyon, gone. And good riddance, Cole thought to himself.

Cole broke cover and nudged his horse out at an easy walk, crossing back over the canyon to the other side.

He followed a dim game trail along the canyon wall,

rounded a hulking hedgehog cactus jutting out from the wall. Suddenly he jerked up to a stop.

Harley!

"What took you so long?" Harley asked casually from where he was squatting in the slim shade of a barrel cactus.

"Thought I'd seen the last of you," Cole said.

"Not likely," Harley said, and stood up. "Picked up sign of a trail rider over yonder. He's protectin' their backtrail."

Cole looked toward the cactus patch Harley indicated. "I doubt if he seen us," Harley added reassuringly. "Sign shows he left more'n an hour ago."

"You really intend to go after them horses, don't you?"

"If I don't, I'd have to answer to Mr. Hamilton. Besides, if I know Mr. Hamilton, he'd have every man in the country chasing after them Indians to get his horses back."

"He would, huh?"

"He hates to lose," Harley answered, looking at Cole cat-eyed.

It was clear to Cole that Harley had made up his mind. "You expect to just ride up on them Indians and get the horses back just like that?"

"Man would be a plumb fool to try that," said Harley. "I figure the both of us could ride ahead of them, wait our chance, and jump them."

"Mister, if that's the way you figure it, have at it," Cole said mildly. "Me, I got my own plan."

"Name's Harley." Harley's eyes held Cole's. "It takes a heap of doin' to outdo an Indian when it comes to stealin' horses. You figure to steal them back alone?"

"I'll get 'em," Cole said, and spurred the bay away, heading out into open plains.

Where Cole rode was gentle-rolling land, a land of cholla and devil's-head cactus, carpeted all around with buffalo grass. And it was a thirsty land.

Soon Cole fell into the trampled path of the horse herd.

Now and again he ranged his eyes far ahead to the left, keeping a wary eye out for the trail rider, looking carefully at places where a man could hide in ambush.

Hours later, slanting in from the right where Cole knew he was, Harley cantered up alongside Cole. "That trail rider crossed in back of the horses. He's scouting to the west now."

"Know that," Cole said. "Indian war trail into Chihuahua over west of here. They'll take the horses where water holes are known."

"You know the country?"

"Some."

Harley knew Cole didn't want him along. So Harley had simply kept his distance from Cole, riding the far flank, but keeping him in sight.

Cole trailing so far behind the stolen horses was stupid, wasting time, Harley thought. Harley wanted to move faster. Get on with it. Twice he had started to strike out on his own, but had changed his mind at the last minute.

Now Harley said patiently; "We was to do some hard ridin', we'd beat 'em to that war trail. Then we could pick our spot."

"Mister, you want to do that, you go right ahead," Cole said stiffly.

"Name's Harley."

Cole looked at Harley. "You'd get there with a played-out horse, then where would you be?"

"Goddammit!" Harley exploded. "Horses is what we're after! We get that horse herd, we can take our pick!"

"If we don't get us killed first," retorted Cole. He paused a long minute, then spoke again: "We'll get the horses. But we'll get them my way."

"Your way!" Harley roared. "The hell you say! Ain't no nig—you ain't givin' me no orders!"

"I won't bother to," Cole said calmly, ignoring what Harley had started to say. Then Cole said knowingly, "When it comes to chasin' Indians, it's best not to hurry. They won't."

"You ain't tellin' me nothin' I don't already know about Indians," Harley said. "But they can be killed just like any other man."

"If this is the bunch I think it is, every warrior there will take some killin'."

"Have it your way!" Harley said, waving a dismissive hand, spurring off to the west at a fast clip.

Riding easy at his own pace, Cole watched him go.

The hard packed ranch yard at MFD was bathed in blistering sunshine. Nobody stirred. All the ranch hands were out on the range. Two chickens scratched at the ground, looking for something to eat next to the bunkhouse door. Frank's roan and two other mares were cropping scrawny grass over in the corral.

A man wearing a bloodstained apron pushed open the bunkhouse door, threw out a pan of water. More out of habit than anything else the man casually lifted his eyes to the north. He was turning in his steps to go back inside when something caught his eye. Facing back around, he looked closer this time.

A man. On a big black horse. And whoever it was was slumped over in the saddle, obviously struggling to get the gate open. Mike!

With the dishpan still in his hand, the cook ran across the yard, heading for the ranch house. His boot heels hit the porch, and he called out, "Mr. Driskill! . . . Mr. Driskill!"

Frank Driskill came to the screen door. "What in hell's all the fuss about, Cookie?"

"Mike's yonder!" He pointed. "Looks hurt!"

Frank looked. He saw Mike slumped in the saddle, the big black horse standing there at the water trough. Frank burst through the screen door, took off at a dead run toward Mike.

"Trouble, Pa," said Mike feebly.

148

"You hurt bad, boy?" Frank asked anxiously.

"Gunshot . . . only a flesh wound." Frank helped Mike get a leg over the saddle horn, then Mike dropped to the ground heavily, wincing from pain when he landed.

"Who did it?" Frank asked, looking at Mike's bloody shirt.

"Stranger. Never seen him before. In the Bon Ton."

"How come?"

"There's talk, Pa." Mike's questioning eyes held his father's. "Talk about us."

"What kind of talk?"

"Your past, Pa . . ." Mike's eyes faltered, looked away at the ground for a second or two, then lifted back to the cook.

"Bring some water, Cookie," Frank ordered.

When the cook was out of earshot, Frank demanded, "Now, say it plain. What's this all about?"

"Pa, there's names to go with that newspaper article. Word is around. It's you, Pa."

Frank's shoulders sagged, as if a great gust of dignity had gone out of him. His eyes were blank, distant.

Mike stared dully at his father. "Pa . . . is Cole . . ."

Mike's voice seemed distant to Frank, a hollow voice from out of the past. And it chilled Frank, sent him cold, rough-edged. "Don't ask, boy!" Frank's fingers dug into Mike's shoulder, his lips drew tight. "Don't ever ask, you hear!"

Mike jerked his arm away roughly. "Then it's true!"

Just then the cook came out the door, returning with the water.

"We best look after that wound," Frank said urgently. "We'll talk later," he added gravely.

"There's nothing more to say," Mike shot back. "Everybody knows already." Mike slumped off, walking toward the bunkhouse, leaving the cook standing there holding the pan of water, perplexed.

"Mike!" Frank called after him. "Come on up to the house. That wound needs looking after."

Mike stopped. "It's only a flesh wound," he said without even turning around to look at his father. "I'll see to it myself."

Anger flushed over Frank. "Mike, you don't understand. There's things you don't know."

"I know all I need to know," Mike snapped. He added pleadingly, "Can't you see, Pa? We can't stay here." Mike cut his eyes toward the cook again, but ignored his presence this time and kept talking. "Ma's heard the talk too," Mike said in a low voice, embarrassed.

"Your ma and me," Frank said stiffly, "we buried the past long ago. What's done is done."

"I can't stay here, Pa!" Mike screamed, choking back angry tears. "I won't!"

"Your ma and me put in a lot of years of blood and sweat drivin' down roots here. We intend to stay."

"What about Ma? What will townfolks say behind her back?"

"We're stayin'," Frank stated definitely.

"And Cole?"

"Cole!" Frank screamed. "Cole is no concern to me," he added, bristling. "The law says he's free to come and go same as you and me."

Mike turned away sharply, moved off a few paces, then slowed down and said over his shoulder, "Ma will be here in the mornin'."

"We'll talk some more then," Frank suggested hopefully.

"I got nothin' more to say," Mike stated bluntly, and kept on walking.

"We'll talk!" Frank yelled at his back.

The Mexican driver handling the lines to the carriage was not his usual talkative self this morning. He had been uncommonly quiet on this trip, silent the whole way, his eyes studiously held on the road ahead of him. Nora could sense that it was a conscious effort on his part, brought on by what he had heard in town.

She sat stiff-backed, her hands clasped together in her lap, her face a mask of stone. She knew Frank was not the sort of man to be run out of the country because of talk. It would take more than just talk to drive Frank out.

Twice she had started to say something to Pico, and twice she had changed her mind. What was there to say? Pico had surely heard the talk. Santa Angela had been buzzing ever since word of the meeting had spread.

The meeting was special. Santa Angela's prominent women had been called together by Nora herself.

Years earlier the women of the town had organized a Women's Auxiliary to tackle the town's social problems.

Led by big-bosomed Emma Teel, the Auxiliary had been effective in keeping rowdies, whores, and thieves in the red-light district. Blacks were kept away too. In the Flat. Twice the Auxiliary had kept legal hangings from public view. "Hang 'em out in the mesquites!" Emma had demanded. And the women had raised funds to build a one-room school for Mexican children. And were now raising funds for a colored school.

This morning's meeting had been held in the schoolhouse. Nora had faced them squarely, speaking mostly at Emma, whose word was listened to. "You all have heard the talk," Nora said honestly. "Now some of you want us to leave. Well, like most of you, me and Frank had hoped to put the past behind us. Build a new community here. Well, we built that community. Now some of you say we're not welcome.

"Today I will ride out to the ranch, talk to Frank. I would like to tell him that the women of the town will stand by us." Nora's eyes held Emma's. "But that is for you to say."

"Nora, just tell us it's not true!" implored Gussy Modkin, sitting on the front bench.

"I have no intentions whatever to trot out my past before the town. Whether you believe it's true or not is for you to say.

"You all know Frank. I can't promise he will abide by your decision." Nora ran her eyes over the women in turn, all seven of them. Then she said pleasantly, "Ladies, I have shopping to do at Haverty's. I'll expect your decision when I return." Nora lifted her chin proudly, departed the room, high-buttoned shoes ringing across the room.

Thirty minutes later, Nora was back. The merchandise she had bought was stacked in back of the carriage parked outside, Pico sitting in the driver's seat, waiting to go.

"Nora, I am sorry," said Emma sympathetically to Nora inside. "There's nothing we can do. You know the town."

"I quite understand, Emma," Nora replied solemnly.

"It's too much to ask of us," said Lydia, a pint-sized whip of a woman.

"Ladies," Nora said with formality, "I shall carry your decision to Frank. I make no promise that he'll honor it. As for me, of course I shall stand by my husband." Nora gathered up her skirts preparatory to leaving. "It's been a pleasure knowing all of you. Good day, ladies," and she nodded politely.

"Nora, I am sorry," Emma said defensively.

"Good day, Emma." Nora turned, walked out the door, mounted the carriage.

Now the carriage wheeled into the sun-splashed ranch yard.

Frank rushed out the screen door, ran across the porch toward the carriage. There was a fixed smile on his lips, a plastered smile showing no warmth whatever. Frank knew trouble was here.

Chapter Thirteen

Ranger Sergeant Ted Armstrong and his partner, Jesus Rivera, sat on crude camp chairs talking across the dest at Captain McNelly. Armstrong looked the part of a drifting grub-line cowpuncher, and Jesus was disguised as a pastore, or sheepherder.

Armstrong was saying, "Me and Jesus was listenin' around like you said, and we snooped out the whole thing right there in the Bon Ton. Morgan's in it hip deep. He had the word sent around about Frank Driskill. And had that Driskill kid set up for a killin'."

"Marshal Ashbel was sent to pull the trigger?" McNelly asked, astonished.

"Naw, Capt'n. The way I figure it, the marshal hightailed it out of here with Burt and Mort, took Morgan's orders over to Santa Angela. Ashbel was the hidden gun. Just in case. He took the first bullet 'cause that kid spotted the setup. The other man shot dead . . . Ike Booker, he was the gun hand. He'd done dirty work for the sheriff before."

McNelly cocked his eyebrows at Armstrong. "You sayin' the sheriff over there . . . what's his name . . . ?"

"Tucker . . . Ralph Tucker."

"You're sayin' Sheriff Tucker was in on it?"

"He's the one Morgan ordered to do it."

McNelly stood up. "Good work, Sergeant," he said. "And you too, Jesus." McNelly scratched at the scraggly hair on his jaw, thinking. "We got a crooked lawman over to Santa Angela, a dead marshal on our hands here, and the county about to bust wide open. Every white man in the territory with a spotted past is jumpy over being found out.

"Some of these men come in here with families and have built homes, reputations. They won't give that up easy. There's bound to be more killin'."

"That's the way it shapes up to me too, Capt'n."

"I'll make my report to Chief Steele. He'll want to know about the goings-on over there at Santa Angela. Investigate maybe."

McNelly looked critically at Armstrong, then Jesus. "Get yo'selfs straightened around, some fresh mounts. We've got more work to do."

"More trouble, Capt'n?" Armstrong asked.

"Juan Cortinas sent his bandits across the Rio Grande last night. Morgan claims they run off three hundred head of Box H beeves. Them rustling this far east, they'll likely gather in every beef between here and the Mes'can border. They'll be slowed some. With some hard ridin', we ought to come up on them out there on the prairie. We move out within the hour."

James Earl Steele, a big square-shouldered, red-haired man, was the state's adjutant general and chief of police. In charge of every law officer in the state.

And just now at the state capitol Chief Steele was sitting

at his desk drumming his heavy fingers over the walnut top, McNelly's lastest report spread out before him, his mind puzzling over what he ought to do about the simmering state of affairs that Captain McNelly had reported.

From McNelly's report the country was primed to blow its lid any minute now. The slightest spark could ignite a race war built on guilt and hate between white men who had lived as neighbors for years.

Chief Steele was a man caught up in a political whiplash of cross-purposes. On the one hand, he was to bring law and order to all citizens. On the other hand, the governor had in so many words ordered him to crack down hard on free-wheeling niggers.

On the one hand, he was to put enough lawmen in the field to do the job. On the other hand, he was to disband the state police, a place of employment and prestige for black Republicans.

Democrats looked upon Steele as a weak, vacillating man unwilling to act with sufficent ruthlessness in their behalf.

Republicans, black and white, had suffered callous, uneven treatment dished out by the chief's lawmen. It was obvious Steele was a stooge for Democrats, a brazen, heavy-footed man with no intentions whatever of administering the law fairly.

Ever since Democrats had taken over the state, Steele had received a steady stream of reports of killings and lynchings in and around Santa Angela. But these killings had been mostly over stock. Now the reports more and more read of revenge killings and lynchings out of hate, fear, and prejudice. Even his unwanted state policemen were at times victims. Steele was brazenly ignoring the killings. His lack of action was conspicious, drawing considerably loud comment from families of victims and from defeated Republicans, particularly ex-senator Ruby.

Chief Steele was uncomfortable with his position, very uncomfortable.

Struck by a thought, Steele stopped his drumming fingers, his eyes staring into the future, his mind sorting over details.

Ten minutes later, Chief Steele was in the office of Senator Mullis, chairman of the Senate Frontier Defense Committee, the committee responsible for legislation on law and order out on the frontier. Zell Biggers was there.

Senator Mullis spoke thoughtfully when he had heard Steele out. "I like your thinking, Chief. Something like this, carried out properly, could benefit us greatly."

Zell Biggers's eyes widened. He was astonished. "Senator, you don't mean it," Zell said quietly. "Morgan won't stand still for this."

"Morgan's had his chance. He'll drag us all to ruin if we don't handle this right."

"From what Captain McNelly reports," Steele said, interrupting, "its a surefire thing, Senator. The country is ripe to blow up any minute. My plan will bring the spark. And after that nobody will be able to hold down the lid. It'll be easy pickin's."

Senator Mullis exchanged looks with Biggers. "Morgan is out," the senator announced definitely. "Unless you want to join him, you keep this between your ears, you hear?"

"I hear," Biggers said quietly, got up, walked out of the room slump-shouldered.

When he was gone Mullis asked Steele, a questioning lift to his eyebrows, "Disarming the coloreds . . . is that liable to cause a loud stir we can't control?"

"Most of them will take it quietly, but some will fight it."

"What troubles you have, take care of them. But keep it quiet. Ruby could make trouble for us.

"You know, Steele," Mullis said thoughtfully, "there's white men who think that everybody ought to be barred from bringing firearms into city limits. I can't say as I disagree with them. But I'm damned if I'll take that tack. Not yet, anyhow.''

Steele was shocked at the mere thought. "Senator," he said resolutely, "there ain't a white man west of the Brazos River who'll give up his pistol willingly. Country's too lawless . . . Outlaws, Mes'can bandits, stock thieves, to say nothin' of maraudin' Indians.''

"The time will come, though," Mullis said. "Mark my word," the senator warned direly. Presently Senator Mullis brightened, said pleasantly, "Let's hope good Democrats still have charge of the statehouse when that time comes, Chief.''

It was late afternoon. Long shadows reached dark fingers across Tubac's main street, a slight breeze in the air. Leg-weary cow ponies stood limp at the hitchrails lining the street. Two men loafed on a bench in front of the sheriff's office.

Four trail-spent men riding slumped over in the saddle walked their horses down the main street, coming in on the road from the north. The men had a striking similarity: They all looked to be fighting men, men who knew what for; and each man was black.

Every man on the street that day knew who they were by the outfits they wore: The state police provided a man a mount, a pistol, and a change of clothes that included a brown canvas bush jacket.

The foursome turned their horses into the hitchrail in front of the sheriff's office. A tall, grim-faced, severe man was the first to step down, wearily. The other three dismounted as a unit.

The tall man rested a hand on the hitchrail, his eyes sweeping the town.

He was a little better than six feet, wore a low-crown black hat. His face was bony, skin like black leather, eyes deep brown, the color of old bark. He appeared to be thirty-five or forty.

When he had looked up and down the street to his satisfaction, he brought his eyes to bear on the two loafers sitting on the bench in front of the sheriff's office. He gave an order to one of his men even as he assessed the two idlers: "Fate, see to the horses."

Fate Elder was a youngster, just turned eighteen. He was a new man on the force.

Fate locked questioningly at the tall man, then, lifting his eyes up the street, asked. "Where, Ples?"

"Stable's yonder," Ples said, nodding.

Ples Butler was an old hand on the job. He had been one of the first colored men hired as a state policeman. He was drawing sergeant's pay now.

Butler was a top-notch lawman, knew his job. And did it. He was a Civil War veteran, had done his share of killing, in and out of the war. Some said he had revenge killings to his credit, too.

The other two lawmen with him on this assignment were Toby Clark and John Lott.

Toby had been doing duty with Ples for four years. They had ridden some long trails together, had come through some tough fights. Twice Ples had dug a bullet out of Toby's body, and once Toby had returned the favor. Most times Toby knew what Ples was thinking before Ples thought of it, especially if Ples had a wrong thought in mind.

Lott was an experienced lawman too. Usually he had command of his own men. Unaccountably he had been assigned under Ples Butler for this job.

None of the four men had any schooling, no education to speak of. Each was just trying to stay alive in a job that had come his way because of the political times and the color of their skin.

Butler's boot heels hit the boardwalk in front of the sheriff's office just as Sheriff Burt Lindley came out the door.

Burt had been put into the deceased Sheriff Ashbel's place by Morgan Hamilton.

Burt took only a cursory glance at the black men and asked thoughtlessly, "Somethin' I can do for you boys?"

Butler ignored the question, walked on by Burt into the office. Toby and John turned sideways and filed silently by Burt stopped in the doorway, entered the office too.

Burt asked at their backs, "I said, is there somethin' I can do for you boys?"

Butler was looking at a row of wanted posters in back of the desk. Still ignoring Burt, Butler walked over, snatched down one of the posters. Turning, he held it up to view. "See this man, Toby?"

A slow second or two Toby studied the picture on the poster, making a big deal of it, then said in mock surprise, "That's John Wesley Hardin!"

Every man in the territory had heard stories about the killing and robbing of John Wesley Hardin. Black folks knew of him because a black peace officer had been sent out to arrest Hardin. Hardin and his gang had horsewhipped the man, sent him packing. Told him it was beneath his dignity to be arrested by a nigger. And that the next nigger, or anybody else for that matter, sent to arrest him would stretch hemp. The authorities took him at his word, so a blind eye was turned to Hardin's lawlessness.

"That ree-ward money looks mighty good," Toby drawled, looking at the offer of a thousand-dollar reward. "Soon as we git a bite to eat me and John ought to ride out to that two-bit horse camp he calls a ranch he's holed up at, and put a bullet in his ass. We'd be back before night." Toby widened his eyes at Butler. "You ain't figurin' on shootin' this here feller," Toby nodded, indicating Burt, "before him, is you?"

"What is this?" Burt blurted out.

"We ought to shoot him first," John said seriously, "rustle up some grub, then go after Hardin. No use in puttin' off killin' one dirty bastard to go after another."

Burt went red behind the ears, lips white. "Who you boys? What you want?" Burt's eyes went over the belt gun each man wore, a government-issue single-action Army Colt. In his mind's eye he took note of the rough cut to their manners and dress. And got unnerved.

"Name's Ples," Butler told him. "Ples Butler, state police." Ples sat a hip on the corner of the sheriff's desk, said conversationally, "I got orders from the state house. You been relieved. Take whatever belongs to you and clear out."

"You can't do this! . . . The town hired me!"

"As of this minute the town is under authority of the state police. And that's us."

Three other wild counties had been run by state police since the late war: Limestone County in east Texas when the settlement of Groesbeck resisted living under the authority of black policemen; Zavala County when a big range war flared out of control over *orejanos*, or unbranded stock, and grazing rights; and De Witt County when the Sutton-Taylor feud raged, claiming lives daily. Ples Butler had been in on the last one.

Burt had heard stories about the state police. He knew their reputation as tough, heavy-fisted lawmen who didn't shy away from killing when it came to that. It didn't take much to provoke a gun battle, somebody had told him.

"The town won't stand for it!" Burt blurted out halfheartedly. "You'll see."

Ples lifted his hip off the corner of the desk, rose to stand, walked behind the desk. Pulled back the chair, sat down. Resting his elbows on the desktop, he put his face in his two hands, glowering out with cold, hard eyes at Burt, his mind working at what he ought to do with him.

Just at that instant, boot heels scraped across the boardwalk, and a boot toe to the rump sent a man crashing across the doorsill.

Ples sprang to his feet, gun hand poised; Toby and John braced in their steps, both men ready for action.

Fate Elder walked through the door, a smirk on his lips. "Ples, liveryman here says he ain't seein' to no nigger horses," Fate said seriously, kneading a bruised right fist in his left palm.

Ples relaxed, dropped back down in the chair, smiling without humor. "You tell him the horses ain't niggers?"

"I told him, but he wouldn't take my word for it."

Ran Johnson, the hostler Fate had just booted into the room, pushed up to his knees, then stood up on his feet, looking around the room for answers.

Burt quickly looked away; Toby eyed him disdainfully; John smiled knowingly.

Ples eyed Johnson contemptuously. There was a big red welt under Ran's left eye, his bottom lip broken on the side, a puddle of blood collected at the corner.

"You think he's convinced now they ain't nigger horses?" Ples asked Fate.

"Well, not really. I brung him along so's you could discuss the matter some more with him."

Ples walked from behind the desk toward Johnson, a stiff draw to his lips. "I'd hate to horsewhip a man out there in the street to get our animals seen after," Ples said pleasantly.

John cut in. "I never heard him say he didn't want to see after our horses. Did you, Toby?"

"Can't say as I did," Toby agreed. "But he looks to be a man who might need some convincing. That right, mister?"

Ples was face-to-face with Johnson now.

Ran's eyes shifted from Burt's back to Ples's.

Ples's voice went harsh. "What about it? Do we get service, or do you need some more convincing?"

"They state police, Ran," Burt said weakly. "You best serve them."

A second or two Johnson hesitated, saying nothing, thinking it over, his eyes sizing up Ples. Johnson couldn't make himself take the chance. "I'll see to 'em," he said submissively, and backstepped to the door, plunged through and away. After a few embarrassed seconds, Burt plunged out too.

Ples shook his head sadly, swore viciously at the prejudice and hatred. "That's what we up against," he warned. "Keep your eyes open. There's a bunch more like them two."

Chapter Fourteen

Harley was miles away from town. He had ridden west bent on beating the Indians to their war trail into Chihuahua and Cole had watched his trail dust fade out of sight.

Cole knew that by riding hard and fast, Harley could outdistance the raiding party. They were moving unhurried, sure of themselves.

The way Cole had it figured, two dangers faced Harley. First, the Indians had a trail rider out watching their backtrail; and second, Harley would be a man alone riding a beat-out mount when he got there, if he got there.

Two hours later by the sun, the tracks of the horse herd, in particular the big Andalusian tracks, had brought Cole to the rim of Woods Draw.

He had cut sign of Harley's passing: a big, long-striding, shod horse. And twice he had seen the unshod hoofprints of the trail rider's pony.

Now Cole sat the saddle, looking along the rim up and down the canyon, studying the terrain.

Woods Draw was an ancient streambed that had simply sunk down from the surrounding country, taking creosote bushes, stunted mesquite, Spanish dagger, and buffalo and mesquite grass with it. It was a sunken desert alone on the prairie, had slanting red-clay walls, a rock-hard red bottom. And precious little water.

The Indians were moving slowly, one Indian wounded— the drag of a crude travois had been seen occasionally out there on the prairie. The Indians were obviously using this route as a diversion to discourage pursuit.

Cole drew the back of his hand across his dry lips, lifted his eyes to the sun, judging the time. Shifting his gaze farther down the draw, he made out a speck of movement against the rugged landscape. That would be Harley.

Indians were first-rate plainsmen. Any one of them would know better than to lose sight of his backtrail by riding down in the bowels of a draw! That was Harley, all right. That trail rider would be riding the rim of the draw where he could see at least a mile in any direction.

Cole swung his horse, skirting the east rim of the draw. At the sight of a dim game trail leading over the rim, he checked the bay to a halt, dismounted. Dropping down on his heels, he studied the immediate vicinity carefully, looking for sign, anything at all.

Mesquite bean!

It was no more than a sliver, a splinter, that caught Cole's eye. But it was something that was out of place, didn't belong with the surroundings.

What Cole saw was the fiber a man spit out when eating mesquite beans.

The mesquite bean is sugary and succulent, loaded with moisture. Indians pound the beans into meal, mix it with wheat flour and make pinole. Or add water to the mix and make atole. But the pod is tough fiber, not fit to digest.

The beans come in mighty handy to a man careful of his water, but he'll spit out the pod.

That trail rider was chewing mesquite beans to conserve his water, spitting out the pods.

Cole turned the sliver over in his fingers, checking for moisture.

None.

But the pod was still flexible, not stiff as it would be if it had been lying out here in the sun for hours.

Cole straightened up, lifted his eyes down the draw.

Nothing moved.

He mounted up, nudged the bay out at a walk, his mind thinking over how best to deal with the situation he faced.

The way Cole figured it, that trail rider was two hours, maybe a little less, ahead of him. And if the trail rider didn't suspect pursuit, he would join the camped band come nightfall, and a nightwatch would be put out.

On the other hand, if he was alerted, he'd simply drop back and kill Harley, then report to the leader of the band, and a tight watch—two, three men maybe—would be put out.

Would Harley's trail dust be spotted, making Cole's task doubly hard? It was a sure thing that if Harley was spotted he was a dead man. The only open-ended question was whether the trail rider would take time to twist Harley slowly over a fire, or kill him out of hand.

An Apache was a notional fighter. How he did his killing depended on his frame of mine, and on his enemy's courage, or lack thereof.

Most troubling to Cole was that if Harley came within seeing distance, that Apache would see him. It was that simple. Apaches could sit like a rock for hours, looking. If anything moved, he saw it.

Cole knew that whatever it was that had moved down there, the trail rider had seen it.

That's just what had worried Cole ever since Harley had come along.

Cole gigged the bay into saddle gait, his eyes scouting the ground in front of him.

A quarter mile farther on he found what he was afraid of: unshod pony tracks. Two smudged hoofprints in a stretch of gravel. A stone disturbed, dark side up.

The tracks were spaced wide apart. The Indian was running his horse!

Harley! Cole spurred his horse, took out.

Farther down the trail he came upon more hoofprints, this time out in the open, running hoofprints.

Abruptly the bang of a rifle racketed back to him.

He raked spurs across the bay's flanks, urging him faster.

Five minutes . . . ten . . . He was riding at a flat-out gallop, scanning the flat country in front of him and occasionally glancing over the rim down in the draw.

Another mile of hard riding, and he made out a horseman ahead.

The trail rider. Riding the rim, leaning low over his pony, shooting at something down in the draw, the dull echo of answering fire of a Winchester rising up out of the draw.

Cole stood in his stirrups, searching his eyes over the rim where the shots were coming from.

Harley!

Harley was riding the graveled bed of the draw, firing his Winchester up to the rim some hundred yards away.

It was clear to Cole that Harley was riding for his life. The Indian commanding high ground had Harley at a fatal disadvantage.

His horse on the dead run, Cole reached back and unsheathed his Winchester, brought it to bear, taking dead aim on the Indian in front of him.

Suddenly the Indian swung his pony, plunged over the

rim, disappeared from sight. Instantly two rapid-fire shots echoed back to Cole.

At a wild gallop Cole reined the bay over the rim, taking the same trail the Indian's pony had plunged into.

Over the edge he went, the bay sliding on its haunches, trying to hold the trail.

The trail down the side of the draw was narrow, only a runoff where water had trickled down from the prairie years ago. The graveled path twisted and turned, doubled back in places, and was overgrown with catclaw and sandbur, slabs of sandstone looming menacingly.

Cole's horse was no wild mustang, as the Indian's had been. But there was no turning back now.

The horse plunged on ahead, front hoofs clawing for solid footing, hindquarters stiffened, braced. Down, down he plunged.

Twice the horse went to his knees, fought back up.

Suddenly he gave out. With an agonized scream, the bay's legs went like jelly. He made one last lunge and went down, head over hindquarters.

Cole had sensed what was coming and had kicked free of the stirrups. Now he jumped from the saddle in a headlong dive, Winchester in hand.

He landed belly-first, skidding down the mountainside like a man being dragged by a wild bronc. Halfway down his body left the trail, ripping headlong through a patch of scrub mesquite, catclaw, and sandburs. Somewhere near the bottom he slammed into a boulder, tumbled head over heels the rest of the way down.

He lay still, his mind going over his body for broken bones.

None, he thought. There was pain in his shoulder and left side, but he felt nothing broken. His face stung from the bushes it had raked over it.

Slowly, carefully, he rolled over, drew his legs under him, pushed up to a squat, looked around.

The Indian was nowhere in sight. Cole's Winchester he had dropped in the fall was twenty yards away. His horse had somehow made it down, and stood trembling, nose flared, eyes wide. The bay saw him, whickered softly, came two steps toward him.

He rose to standing, retrieved his Winchester. Walking toward his horse, he spoke in a low, soothing voice, calming him down.

Just as he got hold of the reins, three quick shots went off, then another, coming from down the draw.

Quickly Cole sheathed his Winchester, swung into the saddle, spurred off.

Away he went, down the draw, swung past a jumble of boulders, arounded a blind bend in the trail. Suddenly he jerked up short, reaching back for his Winchester all the time, his eyes taking in the situation.

Apache! The trail rider. Seventy-five, maybe eighty yards in front of him.

And so was Harley! And Harley was in a fix.

His horse was down. Obviously shot dead on the run, Harley was still in the saddle, struggling to get his left leg from under the dead animal. His Winchester lay ten yards away, his pistol nowhere in sight.

At this moment Harley was helpless, a goner.

The Indian was stalking toward him, a scalping knife in his left hand, a Winchester in the other.

The bay snorted. It smelled blood, possibly.

And that's what alerted the Indian. He whirled around, instinctively crouched low in a fighting stance.

His instinct for fighting is what saved him.

Cole's first bullet zinged over the Indian's head. The next shot was far off the mark, because the Indian had leaped like a scalded cat at the first explosion of Cole's Winchester.

Cole knew before he fired the first shot that it would be sheer luck to hit the Indian at that distance—and him mounted, no less. He only wanted to draw attention away from Harley.

But the Apache had other ideas.

In a half-dozen quick strides he was hovering over Harley. And in one easy motion he touched the barrel of his Winchester pistol-fashion to Harley's head and pulled the trigger. Harley was dead before the echo rose. And just as quickly the Apache's skinning knife flashed, and he lifted Harley's hair in his fist.

Cole jabbed spurs to the bay, closing the distance.

Holding up his bloody trophy, the Indian wheeled in his tracks, dashed to his horse, leaped onto his blanket saddle, and heeled out.

Cole got off a couple of chancy shots, but that was it. The Indian disappeared around the bend.

Cole had the bay in a full-out run when he got to Harley's body. And he kept fogging it. At the bend where the Indian had disappeared, Cole jerked to a skidding stop, jumped from the saddle, Winchester in hand. Dropping down on one knee, he panned his eyes along the west rim of the hollow.

It took him only an instant to pick out the spot. A notch in the rim made by runoff. A boulder had come to rest in the notch now framed in the glare of the sun just dipping over the rim.

Cole snugged the Winchester to his shoulder, sighted carefully, and waited.

Presently the shafts of sun rays were broken, a shadow crept across the boulder. An instant later a rider walked his horse into view, a rifle held in his two hands, ready to shoot.

Cole took up slack on the trigger, caught his breath, squeezed.

The rider jerked in the saddle.

He squeezed again.

169

The rider dropped from the saddle.

Cole stood up spread-legged, the Winchester leveled for another shot at the falling target, if needed.

The twisted, mangled body of the Apache came tumbling down the cliff, crashing through creosote bushes, landed headfirst at the bottom of the draw. Behind him came an avalanche of sand, gravel, and rocks. And a Winchester.

With his Winchester still trained on the Indian, Cole walked up to him, boot-toed the body over.

The Indian was big-chested, stocky. Well-built. Had a raw-hide band looped above each biceps, thongs dangling. Had on an antelope skin headband with the hair side out. His complexion was burnt chocolate, hair long and kinky.

Black Horse's band! Cole swore.

There was no doubt in Cole's mind that this warrior was one of Black Horse's warriors. Undoubtedly Black Horse and his cutthroats had struck in Mexico again. And had taken horses on the way back.

Everybody in the country had heard stories of Black Horse, some exaggerated, but most true. White men called him Nigger Horse in outrage.

The story was that in 1853 a black man named Louis Touvant had come into the country as a scout with Lieutenant Amiel Weeks Whipple's survey party to lay out the most practical and economical route for a railroad from the Mississippi River to the Pacific Ocean. The party was besieged, then befriended, by Apaches. Time passed, and Touvant took himself an Apache woman.

Black Horse was the son of that union.

Whipple's favorable report of the country enticed other white men to take to the southwestern frontier, and ill will soon developed.

Some years later, an Apache camp on Sweetwater Creek was mistakenly attacked by a party of buffalo hunters bent on avenging Comanche-Kiowa depredations. The buffalo hunters killed men, women, and children. Among the dead was Black Horse's mother.

From that day on Black Horse turned savage. Striking alone, Black Horse's way was the way of plunder and death.

His medicine was good. His reputation spread throughout the tribes. He drew to him disgruntled warriors from all tribes on the southwestern plains. Now he had fifteen, twenty warriors—Comanches, Kiowas, and Apaches—all expert horse thieves, vicious killers, unmerciful in torture.

Cole turned away from the dead Apache, walked toward his horse, his mind working at his situation.

He knew he had big trouble if Black Horse and his killers had the Andalusians. Black Horse had rightfully earned a reputation as a cunning, cruel enemy, a man of no mercy whatever.

Cole walked over to his horse, shoved his Winchester in the boot, took a last look over his left shoulder at the body of Harley, his scalp gone, the side of his head laid open like a tunnel.

There simply was nothing he could do for Harley. The buzzards and coyotes would do their work as they had done many times before.

He mounted up. And when his backside met leather, his mind was already made up: The horses he'd been sent after hadn't been fetched yet. He had it to do.

He purred the bay out, heading down the draw, taking up the distance between him and the Apaches that had his horses.

Chapter Fifteen

Word spread fast that the state police had taken over Tubac. The law there was nigger law now. Town folks seethed with hate. White men couldn't tolerate being policed by colored men. Covert acts of violence, threats, and intimidations were delivered against defenseless colored families under cloak of darkness. Santa Angela to the north was no better off. There the killings and intimidations were white against white. The vigilance committee had split into factions, each side retaliating against the other for rumormongering and finger-pointing.

Word got out that Sheriff Tucker had the names of white men who had fathered colored offspring. Tucker was shot four times in the back one dark night that same week.

Frank Driskill's cowhands came in from the range one day, found a scrawled note tacked up on the bunkhouse wall warning them all to clear out.

Newspapers railed about the lawlessness, blaming trifling

coloreds outright or implying they were at the root of the troubles.

Farmers, ranchmen, and freedmen had no voice now. The new governor had swept into office on his coattails businessmen, professional politicians, lawyers, financiers, land speculators, and railroad men.

The Democratic agenda was to expand the rail system, increase freight tariffs, and above all else stamp out lawlessness so that business could flourish. This agenda was larger than any one man, even Morgan Hamilton.

Morgan had staked all on making a killing on land commissions when the railroad came through. Now he was a man left high and dry. The railroad had bypassed Tubac. And Juan Continas had turned loose his *bandidos* on Morgan's stock.

Morgan's prospects had sunk overnight with the swiftness of quicksand.

Now Morgan looked across his desk in the sitting room of his ranch house at Zell Biggers, his mind recoiling at the bad news Biggers had just delivered. "I'll not be shoved aside like this," Morgan snapped, slamming his fist down on the desktop.

"Morgan, it's all out the window now," Biggers said consolingly. "We made our play and came up lacking. I say we let it lay. There's other deals to be made."

Morgan eyed Zell distastefully. "That's always been the difference between me and you, Zell," Morgan said scornfully. He poured himself a stiff shot of brandy from a bottle on the desk, tossed it off in one quick swallow. Continued derisively, conversationally: "You're weak, Zell . . . weak as a newborn kitten. Me, I'll not be shunted aside quietly. Somebody'll pay."

Zell's Adam's apple twitched up. "You make trouble, where'll that leave me?" Zell asked, a nervous twang in his voice. "They'll know for sure how you got word."

"That's your problem," said Morgan, smiling wickedly. "If them mealymouthed politicians up yonder want to play fast and loose, I'll show 'em how it's done."

"Morgan, you start trouble there'll be hell to pay. They won't stand for a double cross."

"The country is already smolderin'," Morgan said ruefully. "Maybe I'll just strike a few matches of my own." Morgan rose, smoothing the velvet folds at the front of his vest, eyeing Zell disgustedly. Without warning Morgan's temper flared: "Get out, Zell! If you won't back my play, I don't need you around! Get out!" Morgan snapped. "Drag your worthless carcass back to that pack of mangy dogs that sent you! You're all of a kind!"

Carl Schurz was sitting in a satin armchair across a wide mahogany desk from President Ulysses S. Grant.

Schurz was a German immigrant who had risen to the rank of general in Grant's Army of the Potomac during the late War Between the States. When Grant had won the White House, he parceled out political plums to his former generals for faithful service.

Absorbed in the business of reconstructing the Southern states, Grant required firsthand, reliable information as to attitudes, and complaisance of the defeated rebels toward the federal government. Thus, General Carl Schurz had been appointed Special Federal Agent to the president.

Schurz had been detailed to make a personal inspection of Southern states to assess their progress in Reconstruction, a necessary step on the path to becoming member states in federal councils again.

Schurz had a heavy shoe-brush mustache that obscured his lips. Only lip hair moved when he spoke.

Now the hair moved and a heavy German accent issued

forth, "Mr. President, Texas is a particularly difficult problem. As a people they are politically recalcitrant and individually hardheaded. The white citizens will never accept freedmen as equals unless forced to do so. They've ratified the Thirteenth Amendment all right and slavery is abolished. But in reality things are little different since Democrats took over. They have ways . . . subtle ways. They want to keep the negras down. That consumes the state. Nothing else seems to matter."

Grant was a blunt, straightforward man. His words usually cut to the heart of the matter as he saw it. "Will the governor enforce the laws?"

Schurz crossed a leg over the other, relaxed back in his chair, his voice instructive. "Mr. President," he said respectfully, "The Republican politician swears by all that's holy that he won't, particularly Senator Ruby. But that is to be expected. You recall Senator Ruby is a nig—a colored man."

Grant's eyebrows lifted. "Are they back to bloody-shirt politics again . . . threatening federal intervention?"

"There might be good cause this time, Mr. President."

"Because of Republican complaints?" Grant asked, surprised.

"Democrats too, Mr. President." Schurz leaned forward in his chair, said confidentially: "I had occasion to meet discreetly with a Mr. Hamilton . . . Morgan Hamilton, a former Democratic supporter of Senator Mullis. Hamilton laid out a plan Democrats have hatched that if carried out will surely demand federal action."

"Rebellious talk?"

"Not exactly. But the Thirteenth Amendment would be ripped to doll rags. The Democrats plan to enact state legislation to disarm all colored men and take away their voting rights in primary elections."

"That's preposterous, General! That's a direct slap in the face of the Constitution."

"Not the way they intend to do it. They've dreamed up something called a poll tax. Mr. President, they'll make that tax so steep, not a colored man in the state will raise it."

"And not a colored man could vote," mused the President, "that it?"

"Exactly," said Schurz resolutely.

Grant stood up, face expressionless, eyes cold. "Those hardheaded Texans! They've been warned to guarantee the colored man's rights." Slamming a clenched fist against the top of the desk, Grant screamed, "Damn rebels don't seem to understand! They lost the war!" Presently he bucked up, braced up his shoulders, continued conversationally: "The governor's people begged me not to interfere in state matters and promised me cooperation. I'll not be made a fool of.

"You get word to the governor that if this deliberate provocation goes forward, I'll have the state back under federal control before he can blink an eye. You make it plain to him that this government will have federal troops at every polling place to see that the colored man gets a right to vote, if it comes to that."

"Yes sir, Mr. President."

"And, General, remind him in no uncertain terms that they lost the war, and that some of the people they would deny the vote to was on the winning side."

"Yes, sir."

"This man you talked to . . . this Morgan Hamilton. What's his stake in this?"

"Swears he only wants to keep things calm so the state can get about the business of rebuilding."

"That's too sensible," Grant said, smiling thinly. "You sure he was a Texan?"

Jack Schwartz's Planters House, a single-story clapboard hotel, was situated directly across the street from Pete Haverty's general store. Unlike the Exchange Hotel, the Planters House had inexplicably attracted a clientele of agriculturists—farmers, grain merchants, hay and feed salesmen, and freedmen—all men of Republican ilk. The sparse lobby of the hotel was the place where such men met for political talk.

It was just about sundown when Senator Ruby and two burly black men armed with shotguns came striding through the door of the Planters House, walked resolutely to the clerk's desk. Ruby's jaws were tight, face grimly serious.

At least fifteen men were already waiting in the lobby, some white, most black; some seated, most standing; some armed, most naked as jaybirds.

Somebody closed the two front doors. Low talk subsided, then fell off to silence. Ruby turned around at the clerk's counter, faced the men, looking out over them patiently.

Satisfied, Ruby nodded. His armed guards moved off, took up lookout positions at the rear door, which opened into the alley.

Ruby collected himself, spoke to the gathering:

"You all have probably heard that I was supposed to go up north. Well, I did. And things look favorable.

"You've all heard the talk about the Greenbacks party. I met with the head of the party, and what we had heard is true. They are men organized to put up candidates who will fight to bring back the dollar bill as the monetary standard, to lower taxes, to promote land for homesteading, and to guarantee voting rights for every man.

"The party chairman welcomed our interest, and assured me that if we start a party here, the power and influence of the national organization will be at our disposal."

"What about the Republican party?" a man shouted.

"The last election was a sound rebuke to the Republican party," Ruby answered. "We didn't elect a single candidate."

Ruby stroked his chin thoughtfully. "We've got to change

our label. Whether Greenbacks or Republicans, we'll stand for the same things. We'll put up candidates throughout the state—"

Suddenly a pistol went off.

A man was slammed against the back door. The door splintered, the man crashed across the threshold, dead.

A shotgun boomed from down the alley.

A pistol answered.

Somebody moaned from just outside the door, out of sight. Silence.

The man moaned again.

The men in the lobby knew Ruby's guards had been disposed of, the meeting broken up. "Everybody stay calm," Ruby said, wagging calming hands. "No need for this to turn into a shootin' match!"

"I ain't goin' to stand here and be shot down like a cur dog!" Ira roared. "We got guns! Let's use 'em!"

"No need for that, Ira," Ruby cautioned, walking toward the rear door, now in total darkness. "Let me—"

"You men in there!" came a shouted voice from the street out front. "You got ten seconds to break up that meeting and go on home!"

The men inside could hear muffled hoof-falls of walking horses, but nobody had any idea how many they were. "Who is it?" Ruby asked out, cocking his head to the closed door. "What you want?"

"Makes no never mind! Just clear out of there! You got five seconds and countin'!"

"I'm Senator Ruby! And this is a lawful meeting! We got a right!"

"You mean has-been Senator Ruby," the man retorted, and chuckled derisively. "You got no rights, here!" The man paused, then asked approvingly, "That right, Zell?"

Zell Biggers squirmed uncomfortably in his saddle next to the man doing all the talking.

Morgan had bullied Zell into going along with his plan. But Zell desperately wanted to be somewhere else. He stilled himself and called out unsteadily into the hotel: "That's right, Ruby! This meeting is unlawful . . . highly unlawful!"

"You heard the man!" the voice warned. "Now, clear out! Or else!"

Silence from inside.

"Jack!" the voice called from the street. "Jack Schwartz! you in there!"

"I'm here, Burt! Recognize your voice. And I got me a guess who's with you."

"You get them niggers outa there, Jack! If you don't, there won't be enough left of your hotel to start a kindlin' fire with. You been—"

"I say this is a lawful meetin'," a resolute voice said from behind the men in the street.

The men in the street looked around, found the source of voice behind them.

Ples Butler!

"I'm the law!" Butler said. At his side was Toby Clark. Each man had a pistol belted on and was palming a Winchester, ready for action. "You men leave them alone. Or the only fire you'll see is the one that's burnin' in hell."

Burt Lindley and his men were surprised to see the two lawmen at their backs.

Ples kept his Winchester leveled forward, his eyes taking in the mounted men, trying to place the ones he had seen before. With Burt and Zell were Ned Potter, Ran Johnson, Bill Drake, and two rough-looking cowhands, obviously brought along to do the dirty work.

Ples looked them over carefully, making a mental note of each, then said, "Town's open to lawful gatherin's. I aim to see to it. You men ride."

"This is the town's business," Burt snapped. "Not

your'n. Zell here can vouch that the meetin' is unlawful. Ain't that right, Zell?''

Zell was white around the ears. His voice trembled, "Th-that's right. Jack . . . Mr. Schwartz agrees with me. . . ."

Ples eyed Zell coolly, distrustfully. Then he called inside the hotel, "Schwartz . . . Jack Schwartz!"

"I'm here!"

"Man out here says your hotel is closed to meetin's! That right?"

"Hotel's open to any I say, and I say it's open!"

Biggers suddenly wanted to puke. He raked a tongue over his white lips. Ran Johnson stiffened in his saddle, his temples jumping. Drake and the two other cowpunchers slouched confidently, waiting for the right moment.

For a long minute everything was quiet.

A woman laughed out loud seductively down at the saloon, and a man yahooed.

Ruby yelled through the wooden doors, "Ples! This is Senator Ruby! I'm coming out to talk! We don't want no trouble!"

Burt shot a glance over to Drake, looked knowingly at the two cowpunchers. Burt had been sent here to carry out a plan laid out for him. And had been told not to fail.

Ruby pushed open the door, stepped into the doorway. The light at Ruby's back framed him perfectly, and Burt saw his chance.

"Get him!" Burt screamed, and went for his gun.

Burt's gun never made it up.

Ples shot him. Tore out the back of his skull.

Burt's horse had spun away, putting Burt's back to Ples. Ples had already taken up slack on the trigger, but hesitated a split second. But when Burt's gun started to come up at Ruby, Ples had no choice. Burt's head exploded, and almost at the same time another bullet from Fate Elder's Winchester broke into Burt's chest. Burt left the saddle. Died on the way to the ground.

Toby Clark had seen Ples in action long enough to know that Ples always went first for the man he faced, so Toby's eyes had been on Ran Johnson all the time.

When Burt had made his play, Ran had reached for his gun.

Johnson never made it either.

Toby simply pulled the trigger on his Winchester at point-blank range. Ran Johnson never had a chance.

What Burt hadn't known was that John Lott and Fate Elder had taken up positions behind the facade on top of Pete Haverty's hardware store. When Burt went for his gun, Lott and Elder cut loose.

Lott's first shot dug into Ned Potter's chest, knocking him into the dust. His horse took out up the street.

Fate's second shot only dusted Drake, off the mark in the wild scramble that was on.

Now the scene down in the street was pure pandemonium. Guns roared, men screamed, horses reared and pitched, hot lead zinging all over the place.

The punchers were good horsemen. They all three had wheeled their mounts away, rode up the street. Keeping low in the saddle, they fired at Ruby standing in the doorway. A shot from Drake had knocked splinters from the doorjamb no more than two inches from Ruby's face.

Ruby whirled, leaped back inside. Another man's bullet drilled Ruby in the shoulder, knocking him back clear across the floor.

The three cowboys took turns at their work. Riding low over their horses' manes, the men wheeled their mounts in a tight circle, raced back in range of the open hotel door, fired, then spurred off.

Fate Elder and John Lott on top of the hardware store took

potshots at them as best they could, but it was a chancy thing in the dim light.

By this time Ples and Toby had scrambled under cover behind the water trough between the hotel and the Golden Eagle Saloon.

"Cover me!" Ples ordered Toby.

"What you goin' to do?"

"Get him," Ples said, nodding his head, indicating Zell Biggers.

Zell's horse was standing in the alley next to the bank, Zell frozen stiff in the saddle, hands held to the sky, face ghostly white with horror. Zell knew that orders were to break up the meeting, but he hadn't expected this!

At the first shots, Zell had heeled his horse away, taking himself out of danger.

"Go!" Toby yelled to Ples, and triggered his Winchester at the cowboys as fast as he could work the action.

Ples skittered back from the water trough, got his feet under him, and took off running low across the street. He got to the other side, drew up at the corner of the bank, flattening his body against the wall. His breath came in great gasps as he craned his neck around the edge of the building, eyes searching.

Biggers was still sitting in the saddle there, frozen stiff.

Ples stepped up on the boardwalk, flattened his body against the front of the building. Taking cautious steps, he moved toward Zell, his Winchester ready.

Ples stepped down off the boardwalk. Zell looked over, eyes bulged, lips white. "I . . . I had nothin' to do with it. . . . It was all a mistake!"

In one quick burst Ples lunged, shot a hand up, grabbed Zell by the coat front, and snatched him from the saddle.

"It was a mistake, all right," Ples said, gritting his teeth. "And you goin' to fix it!" Wrenching Zell around, Ples took hold of his coat collar at the back. Throwing aside his Winchester, Ples drew his pistol, cocked it, pointed it in Zell's ear. "Move!" Ples ordered, shoving Zell ahead of him into the street.

Toby saw what Ples was doing. Swore under his breath. Held his fire, then signaled to John and Fate to do the same.

It took only a second for Drake and the cowboys to realize that firing had stopped, that something was up. One by one they reined in their horses, guns held poised, eyes searching for what was up.

Then they saw Zell and Ples out in the middle of the street, Zell being used as a shield.

But Drake was having none of it. He drew up his face in disgust. "That lily-livered weasel!" Drake sneered. "Damn him!" And Drake slapped spurs to his horse, came charging. On cue, the other two men did the same.

Ples saw them coming.

So did Zell. He waved his hands frantically, pleading, his voice carrying in the street. "No! . . . No, Drake! Don't!" He screamed.

In an angry, heedless charge, the three men bore down on Zell and Ples in a full-out run, firing as they came.

Drake's shot ripped into Zell's chest, lifting him back. Two more bullets tore into his stomach. Zell was slammed back against Ples.

Ples let go the coat collar, slung an arm around Zell's waist, holding him upright as a shield, his gun hand free, picking a target.

The cowboys charged on, still shooting. Thirty yards away, Zell's body was still taking lead.

Ples fired. Drake left the saddle. His horse swerved violently to avoid smashing into Ples holding up Zell's body.

And then the other two horses were on top of Ples. He hit the ground on his back, pulling Zell's body on top of him.

He saw a flash of slashing hooves coming at him. But at the last instant the hooves left the ground, soared over him.

And in midair the rider threw a shot. A bullet dug a spout in the dirt next to Ples's head, and the hooves landed, shoveling back dirt in his face.

Flat on his back in a cloud of dust, Zell's body on top of him, Ples fired where he thought the rider would be.

Missed. And the rider was away. Another horse's hoof pounded by his face, throwing back dirt in his eyes.

Suddenly it was over. In seconds.

Toby had got off two quick shots. To no avail.

Ples lay quietly for a long while. Then he rolled Zell's body away from him, stood up, started dusting himself off, eyes checking the street.

The street was quiet, brooding. Trail dust falling back to earth. From somewhere up by the livery a dog barked. Heads appeared at windows, poked out doors. Music from the Golden Eagle started back up again.

Ples saw Toby start walking toward him from up the street. John and Fate showed themselves on the other side of the street, Fate limping slightly from his leap off the building.

Ples holstered his pistol, his mind working over what had just happened.

Before the sun had disappeared behind the horizon, Ples Butler had pieced together the full details of the incident for his report.

Four men had died in the street. Two were wounded: Drake was only winged; his fall from the saddle had knocked the wind out of him. Ruby had a nasty shoulder wound.

Now the lawmen were back in the office, Drake behind bars. John was saying, "Ples, Drake swears Mr. Hamilton called the play. You figure to arrest him?"

Ples lifted his eyes from the report he was writing out.

"Because of Mr. Hamilton the town's got four men to bury. You boys better git some sleep. Come tomorrow, Mr. Hamilton will answer . . . one way or the other."

"You figure us to go after him?"

"Naw. He'll come to us."

Chapter Sixteen

As he approached the carriage, Frank's eyes found Nora's. The smile left his lips. The look on Nora's face told him that the past they wanted to buried had been dug up, had to be rehashed again. It pained Frank to even think about it. He had no stomach for it.

He reached both hands up, swung Nora to the ground. "Frank, we've got to talk," Nora said, landing.

"Plenty of time for that," said Frank cheerily. "Pico, see to the horses, then tell Cookie to rustle up some grub for the house."

Guiding Nora by the elbow, Frank led her toward the ranch house.

Like most ranchmen Frank displayed little compassion. He had no patience for the gentle ways of womenfolk. The country molded a man to be straightforward, direct. Most men out here would just as soon walk ten miles in run-down boots than show tenderness.

"Mike's fine," Frank said gaily, anticipating Nora's concern. "Only a scratch."

But Nora brought him back to the reason for her being here. "It won't just go away, Frank. The trouble Mike had in town . . ."

"Expect not." They went up the steps, walked across the porch.

"We've got to decide," Nora said seriously.

"Decide what?"

Frank drew back the screen door. Nora went through, faced around to Frank, who had just stepped through, her eyes probing Frank's. "The town won't stand by us, Frank. There'll be more trouble."

Frank's eyes were steady, his voice firm, unyielding. "We built this ranch out of wilderness, and not without hardships. What's done is done. I reckon we'll go on right here, come trouble or not."

"I don't know, Frank," Nora said, unsure of her feelings. "The town is so . . . so malicious, so hateful."

Boot heels sounded on the porch. Mike walked in, face solemn. "Mornin', Ma," he said with feelings. ". . . Pa."

"Hello, Mike," Nora answered brightly.

"Morning, son," Frank answered. "Sit down over here next to your ma. You don't look the worse for wear and tear," he added, trying to perk Mike up.

"I'm feelin' fine, Pa," Mike said, walking into the breakfast nook and pulling out a chair at the small table spread with bacon, eggs, biscuits, and coffee that the cook had put out. "Heard Jim ride out this mornin' before daybreak," Mike said. "What's he up to?"

Frank looked at Nora over the rim of the steaming-hot cup of coffee he was holding to his lips. "Reckon you'd hear sooner or later," he said to her. "So I might as well tell ya." He took a small sip, set the cup down. "One of the boys come in from carousin' over to Tubac. Says the town is less

than a hellhole now. Killin's most every day.'' Frank cut his
eyes over to Mike. ''Folks blame it on nigger law.''

Mike's eyes dropped down to the tablecloth, and Frank
continued, ''That's Morgan's bailiwick, so I sent Jim to have
a look-see.''

''What's Morgan got to do with it, Pa?''

''That gunman you faced . . . Morgan sent him after you.''

''What for?''

''Only reason I can figure is to get back at me.'' Frank
glanced over at Nora. ''Morgan's the one bad-mouthin' our
past.''

''And Jim went alone?'' Nora asked, wide-eyed.

''He's got strict orders to stay clear of Morgan. Just look
and listen. I'll deal with Morgan myself when the time
comes.''

''When'll that be, Pa?'' Mike asked angrily.

''In due time. There's no hurry.''

''There is for me,'' Mike said, setting his coffee cup down
hard, rattling the saucer. ''I'm leaving.'' He drew up straight,
stiff-backed.

''When did you decide this?'' Nora demanded, surprised.

''I didn't,'' Mike said. ''You and Pa did.''

''That's nonsense! We never—''

Abruptly Frank shoved back from the table, jumped up,
talking all the while. ''I've tried to talk some sense into him,
Nora! Now I see it's no use. Anyways, it's his decision.
We're stayin'.'' Frank walked away from the table, went into
the hallway, started pacing.

''Mike, you can't mean it,'' Frank heard Nora say aloud,
pleading. ''Your father needs you.''

''He don't need me,'' Mike snapped. Then, in almost an
afterthought, he said, ''Maybe he needs Cole.''

Nora's hand flew up to her mouth; Frank whirled in his
steps, his face livid with fury. ''That's enough, Mike!'' he

screamed from the doorway. "I'll not have it! Not another mention of Cole's name, you hear!"

Mike's chin fell, his eyes studying the tabletop. "Sorry, Ma," he said weakly.

"That's better," Frank said. Frank softened a bit, his tone pleasant when he said to Nora, "Best we let this whole thing rest till Cole gets back. Then we'll settle it once and for all."

Nora could read in Frank's eyes that his words were more a question than anything else. She looked pleadingly at Mike, then said agreeably, "All right, Frank. It can wait." Nora's eyes still searched Mike's, looking for concurrence.

Mike's chin stayed down, only his eyelids visible, his lips silent.

"It can wait . . . can't it, Mike?" Nora asked tenderly.

"It can wait," Mike mumbled grudgingly.

Cole had followed a faint game trail along a narrow stream skirted on both sides by a dense growth of young cottonwoods at the foot of Santiago Mountain. Now he swung the bay into the only clearing he had come across, pulled to a halt next to a bunch of tules at the water's edge, and dismounted.

The Indian's camp was close. Awfully close. He could feel it in his bones. Hair on the back of his neck prickled.

But it had gotten dark.

A million stars twinkled down, the moon throwing out a brilliant glow, lighting up the surroundings.

From higher up a coyote wailed sorrowfully. The gentle night breeze jiggled cottonwood leaves, bent the tules.

He had been following tracks of Black Horse's band for hours now. Miles back they had led him out of Woods Draw. The Indians were moving more cautiously now. They had cunningly ridden out of the draw where the ground was solid rock. He had had to backtrack twice before he found where hoofs had scraped over rock, giving him the general direction.

Alert for sign, anything at all, he had followed more by instinct than anything else. But he knew the Indians would make night camp soon. In the shelter of a mountain valley, probably along this streambed, he figured. And since he had killed their trail rider, Cole knew they'd have at least a double night guard, maybe more.

He knew it was foolhardy, inviting death to proceed on horseback, in darkness, in strange country.

He dismounted. Looking his horse over, he stroked the horse's neck, the only horse he had actually owned himself. He said softly, "I'll find you when this is over." The horse looked around at him, whickered as if he understood what was said.

Stripping off his saddle gear, he slapped the horse's rump, sending him on his way along the edge of the bushes next to the stream.

He had no choice and he knew it. A lone man on horseback in Apache country was simply asking for it. And Cole knew this was no time to make stupid mistakes. Because one mistake out here was all he'd get.

He sat down on a rock next to the stream, tugged off his boots, pulled on the moccasins and knee-high leggings he had taken from the dead Apache back at Woods Draw.

It was at least midnight now, he guessed. He waded across the stream, came out on the other side, ducked under a low-growing willow tree, weaved his way through Pinchot junipers and a scattering of manzanita trees growing in the small valley.

At a big rock at the base of Santiago Mountain he stopped, dropped his saddle, leaned on the rock, catching his breath, checking his backtrail.

Nothing back there except tules fluttering gently in the mountain breeze. He panned his eyes ahead up the slope, looking for the most likely place the Indians might camp.

Nothing obvious.

A coyote called. Another answered. From down by the stream, a night owl screaked.

And then he saw it! A saddle in the mountain ridge. A notch just barely discernible at night and at this distance. Searching his eyes around farther, he discovered a dim trail heading up toward the notch.

Quickly he picked up his saddle gear, slung it over his shoulder. Winchester in his right hand, he moved out quietly, straining up the steep, clumsy trail, his eyes searching the way for sign, anything at all; his ears reaching out for sound, anything at all other than usual night sounds.

An hour . . . two hours Cole walked, his strength and stamina answering the challenge of that craggy, scrub-infested trail that twisted and turned its way up the mountainside.

Now he was a hundred yards away from the pass. He hunkered down in the shadows of a bunch of scrub oaks, surveying the notch, the only pass over the mountains.

Twice he'd had to backtrack and pick another way. Three times he'd had to stop and gather his wind.

He knew that Black Horse and his marauders had gone through this pass. And camped in the valley beyond, they'd have a lookout here.

A million stars still winked down. The moon glowed brilliance, as though it were radiating from the notch itself.

But Cole had observed on the climb up that every now and again clouds scudded over, shrouding the moon, briefly casting darkness over the surroundings. That was the only time he dared move. Even at that, it was chancy.

Moving deliberately, he hid his Winchester out of sight inside his saddle blanket, slid the bundle under some low-hanging scrub oak branches. And just as deliberately he stretched out on his belly, eyes riveted ahead at the notch, waiting for a blanketing cloud to move over.

It was slow going, waiting for clouds to come over, dimming the moon. Two hours later he was still at it, flat on his belly under cover of a manzanita tree no more than twenty yards off to the side in the pass.

Three times moving cloud cover had allowed him to sneak ever closer. He had been in his present position for ten minutes now. His eyes had probed every square inch of the notch.

A sentry was there, all right. Sitting on his haunches motionless as a stone, completely blended in with the slab of rock he was squatting on.

But Cole knew he needed darkness one more time to make his final move. To attack the sentry. So he waited. Stone quiet. His mind working at what must be done.

Suddenly a cloud scudded across the edge of the moon, plunging Cole's position into darkness.

Almost without thinking, Cole jumped up, dug moccasined toes into the gravelly slope, and shoved off in one quick burst like a man leaving the starting blocks.

Three strides . . . five strides; six . . . eight. He was closing fast on the sentry. And then a pebble rattled, and rattled again, rattling another pebble . . . then other pebbles! The sentry jerked around sharply toward Cole, Winchester swinging around to shoot.

Cole's feet left the ground. One hundred and eighty pounds soared through the air as if shot from a bow, slammed into the Indian like a ton of bricks.

Cole had only his pistol, which he dared not use. So he grabbed a handful of Indian, two handfuls.

Over the rock slab they plunged and landed in a wild tangle in a sandpit on the other side.

The Indian was big, heavy-shouldered, solid. Cole's flying impact and landing on top of him had stunned him some. His Winchester had been knocked from his hands.

Now he was doubly dangerous. He shot a foot up into

Cole's crotch, kicked up viciously, launching him head over heels.

Pain swept over Cole, and he came crashing down on his back in the sand.

The Indian had been repelled himself into a rolling somersault. Now he sprang to his feet, crouched low, hands spread wide, coming after Cole, a skinning knife in his right hand.

Cole scrambled to his feet, saw the knife.

Cole still had his pistol, but he dared not use it.

The Indian advanced, stalking like a big cat ready to pounce, looking for an opening, knife held low, blade up.

Cole circled right, keeping away from the blade.

Suddenly the Indian lunged, uppercutting savagely with his blade. Cole easily sidestepped the upslash; the Indian flailed out with a left slap, swishing air harmlessly.

Cole circled away warily. He knew that last slash was only a probing attempt, the Indian only checking out Cole's fighting ability.

But Cole had been checking out the Indian's skill, too.

Now he crouched even lower, stopped circling, eyes riveted on the blade, waiting for an attack, every muscle alert to strike back.

The Indian feinted a stab, then feinted again. Both times Cole's left hand swept down, flicked the wrist away from his body, even as he kept circling.

Now the Indian attacked all out, intending to finish Cole off. He lunged, lashed out a low wicked stab at Cole's belly. Cole sidestepped, shot out a left hand, and caught the Indian's blade hand by the wrist coming in. And in the same motion threw a chopping right that caught the Indian a glancing blow alongside the ear.

The Indian whipped his left leg around, lashed Cole in the bend of his right knee.

Cole was whiplashed, thrown backward. He grabbed a handful of the Indian's hair, taking the Indian down with him, his left hand still gripping the Indian's knife hand. He smashed his knee into the Indian's stomach. When they hit the ground, he shoved up his legs to full length, sending the Indian flying.

He scrambled to his feet, was looming over the Indian when he started to get up. Cole lashed out with a moccasined toe, smashing the Indian's jaw.

The Indian was obviously hurt, in a daze. But he somehow made it to his knees, started to get up again. Cole cracked him alongside the noggin with his pistol barrel, knocking him out cold.

Working swiftly, Cole stripped the Indian of his sheath, recovered the knife, then dragged the unconscious Indian out of plain sight. Retrieving his Winchester and blanket, he mounted the Indian's pony, which he found hidden in the rocks, and heeled away at a quiet walk.

At a gentle incline on the other side of the pass, he checked the pony to a stop, surveyed his surroundings.

Cole didn't know it, but this was Cuesta del Burro, a mountain valley where wild burros came to feed on the lush wheat grass. Mountain peaks sheltered it on the east and west, and a stream from the Santiago Mountain kept the wheat grass lush.

And that's where Cole found Black Horse and his raiders camped.

Cole studied the campsite carefully.

In the moonlight he could barely make out dim circles of ashes of at least four dead campfires, sleeping warriors haphazardly sprawled out around spent fires, their warhorses leg-hobbled off to the side.

A gentle breeze from the mountain peaks caressed the valley, tickling the wheat grass. From higher up a night owl called. Off to his left a horse blew.

Cole shifted his attention there, searching for life.

The horse herd! In a gentle swale south of the sleeping

camp was the horse herd, guarded by one Indian on horseback.

Cole slid from his pony's back, landing silently on moccasined feet, eyes holding fast on the night guard.

He picked his way upwind of the Indian, backtracking and worming his way from bush to shadow, getting between the Indian and the sleeping camp, the least likely direction an attack would be expected.

For a moment or two Cole lay out of sight in the shadow of a scrub oak. Then he stood, walked away from the bush, heading toward the mounted night guard, saddle blanket slung over his shoulder Indian fashion, gun hand gripping his Winchester under the blanket. Just in case.

Cole was within spitting distance of the Indian before the Indian saw him. Cole grunted huskily, waved a careless hand as if he had something to say. And before the Indian could draw his next breath, Cole sprang at his throat.

Off the horse both men tumbled. They hit the ground, landing on the other side, Cole on top of him, a rawhide thong around the Indian's neck. He had taken the thong from the goatskin water bag of the unconscious Indian back in the pass.

In one savage twist of the thong the Indian's wind was choked out of him without a whimper.

The Indian's horse had snorted, shied away. The other horses milled restlessly, ears pricked forward.

For a brief second, Cole lay still on top of the Indian's body, listening into the night, waiting for the horses to settle down.

Everything got quiet.

He stood up, looking around.

Nothing. Quietly, slowly he choused the horses down the swale away from the camp.

A quarter mile or so away he bunched the horses in a

shallow draw and looked them over closely for the first time.

Only one Andalusian in the bunch!

He swore under his breath. Where was the other one?

Black Horse had it!

Chapter Seventeen

Chief Steele's plan was working perfectly. Killing such a prominent man as Zell Biggers set off howls for action heard all the way to the state house.

Steele now had clear-cut justification and the backing of prominent citizens and politicians to rid the state of the hated nigger-packed state police.

Counting on the reputation of Captain McNelly, Chief Steele issued the following order in a dispatch to Ranger headquarters: THE DISREGARD FOR LAW AND ORDER BY THE STATE POLICE IN YOUR DISTRICT CANNOT BE TOLERATED STOP YOU ARE FORTHWITH ORDERED TO DISBAND THEM STOP TWO DAYS HENCE DISARM ALL COLOREDS STOP.

The telegraph operator in Tubac knew firsthand the heavy-footed reputation of Ples Butler and his men. After he had copied down the message and had studied the words more closely, he whistled through his teeth. "Whew! By Jesus this'll really raise hob!"

Meanwhile, Morgan had no inkling that the state police

was on the eve of dissolution. To Morgan's mind, his plan was working. The townspeople were outwardly primed for action against the black lawmen, action he knew would spark federal intervention.

Intervention would roll back the election results, cast out Senator Mullis and other politicians hostile to his interests, and with the same stroke sweep Frank Driskill from the country.

The way Morgan saw it, the situation needed only one final shove, and he intended to give it that decisive push.

Tubac's main street lay quiet in the sun like a wet bullwhip waiting to be snapped. A wide swath of sunlight bathed the west side; a narrow ribbon of shade traced the boardwalks on the east side. Two horses hitched in front of the telegraph office stood head down, waiting for riders. A man led his horse out of the livery, mounted up, and clattered out of town southbound. It was no more than eight o'clock in the morning, but it was already hot. Mighty hot.

Presently the pound of hoofbeats of a lone rider running his horse echoed against the false-fronted buildings. A man jerked to a skidding stop in front of the jail. He dismounted on the run, plunged through the door of the jail. "They comin', Ples," Fate announced breathlessly.

"How many?" Ples asked, reaching for his Winchester propped against the desk. With his left hand he put on his hat taken from the desktop.

"Ten . . . twelve maybe."

Ples looked fondly at Fate and said pleasantly, "How old did you say you was, Fate?"

"I told you, goin' on eighteen."

"Like I told you, jail's goin' to need watchin' whilst I'm out there."

"No use in me stayin' in here," Fate said. "If they kill

you, they'd sure as hell come in here after me."

"Cursing like that," Ples said, "you figger that makes you full-grown, do you?"

"It ain't that."

"What, then?"

"I'd feel better earnin' my wages same as you."

"You ain't exactly got to, you know," Ples said, spinning the cylinder of his pistol, checking the loads, then jamming it back in the holster.

"Maybe they'll back down if they see us both out there," Fate said, brightening.

"I don't 'spect them to," Ples said honestly. "There'll be shootin'."

"Just remember what you told Toby," Fate said.

Toby had earlier reminded Ples to watch his temper and not go off half-cocked. Toby knew Ples would at times shoot first if need be and ask questions later of the dead.

Now Ples slammed back the action on his Winchester, jacking a round into the chamber. "Fate, any man'll listen a whole lot better with a boot in his rump or a gun in his ear."

Dull thuds of trotting hoofs on hard-packed earth reached into the jail. "I'm goin' out," Ples said matter-of-factly. "You can come or stay." And he walked toward the door.

"I'm comin' too," Fate said at his back, following him out.

Ples walked across the boardwalk, stepped off into brilliant sunlight, moved out into the street, Winchester held in his two hands, eyes searching faces down the street.

Morgan Hamilton. And a dozen men sitting their horses in a loose knot in the middle of the street. Hamilton, Kelly, Will Howser, Juan Cortinas. He even had town men with him—Pete Haverty, Lynus. They all sat their horses twenty yards in front of Ples, waiting.

Ples brought his eyes on Morgan. "Been expectin' you."

"Then you know why I'm here. Bring him out."

"Can't do that. Drake's charged with murder. And you charged as his accomplice."

"Me? Charged?" Morgan smiled without humor. "You got the shoe on the wrong foot, pot likker. You're goin' to hang for the murder of Zell Biggers. In the meantime, you just get Drake out here. Or we'll go in and get him."

"I wouldn't if I was you," Ples said mildly.

"You and that kid there goin' to stop us?"

Ples lifted his eyes to the facade over Pete Haverty's store and called, "John!"

John Lott's Winchester barrel was the first thing that came into view, then John showed himself.

Ples shifted his eyes to the far outside corner of the Golden Eagle Saloon. "Toby!" Ples summoned.

Toby stepped away from the corner, his Winchester held ready for action.

"Toby!" Ples called out again. "You and John take off them badges and throw 'em out in the street. You too, Fate."

All three men did as they were told.

Ples looked directly at Morgan. He took off his own badge, tossed it in the street in front of him. "We ain't state police no more."

"That's more like it," Morgan said, smiling knowingly. "Didn't think you boys was foolish enough to lay down your lives over a small matter like this." He rose in his stirrups, said to the men around him, "There's a white man in that jail. I say we let him out."

"You jest go right ahead," Ples replied.

"Kelly, go let Drake out," Morgan said.

Kelly swung his right leg over the cantle of his saddle to dismount. His boot toe touched the ground.

Ples shot him dead. Kelly hit the ground like a sack of grain. Toby swore under his breath.

"That was a damnfool thing to do!" Morgan said, astonished. "You had no right."

Ples swung his Winchester on Morgan. "If you was to catch the next bullet there ain't no law within miles to give a damn."

"Now, look here, you—"

A clatter of hoofbeats sounded behind Ples. Ples looked back over his shoulder just in time to see the man who spoke. The man said in a thin voice that carried in the street, "You men hold it right there!"

McNelly! And four more Rangers. Plus one other man. They pulled to a stop, and McNelly started talking from the saddle, looking at Ples. "Ples Butler, is it." McNelly's words were more a statement than a question.

"That's right."

"Morgan," McNelly said, shifting his eyes to Hamilton.

"I want these men jailed," Morgan said hurriedly. "They got no authority here and killed a man. I want 'em jailed!"

"Butler!" McNelly called out. "Get your men off the street!"

Ples didn't answer. Carelessly he swung his rifle barrel in the general direction of the Rangers.

"I'll deal with Morgan," McNelly said reassuringly.

"He's involved in a murder," Ples said. "And I aim to see he answers."

McNelly spoke without emotion. "My name's Captain McNelly, Texas Rangers. I'd take it kindly if you'd point that rifle somewheres else."

Ples reluctantly moved the barrel of his Winchester.

McNelly continued, "Morgan's right, Butler. Word come down from the statehouse this morning. You out of a job. Get your men off the street or I'll treat the lot of you as common outlaws."

"What about him?" Ples nodded at Morgan. "You coverin' for him?"

"Any other time I'd kill you for that," McNelly said, glowering at Ples. "Anyhow, I'll handle Morgan. Now, take your men and wait for me in the jail. There's somethin' you ought to know.''

When Ples and his men had gone, McNelly resumed talking, speaking conversationally, his eyes on Morgan. ''We caught up with them Mes'can bandits that made off with your beeves, Morgan. After we got 'em back one of the boys butchered one for supper.''

Morgan squirmed uncomfortably in his saddle, raked his tongue over dry lips. ''Well . . . wouldn't hold that against you, Captain,'' he said, unsure of himself. ''Men got to eat,'' he added nervously.

''Trouble was, the underside of the hide showed the brand had been blotted. Sam here,'' and McNelly jerked a thumb at the man sitting his horse next to Armstrong, ''is a brand inspector. Way he figures it, you burned over BAR E critters with your BOX H brand.''

''That ain't so!''

''Sam here, he skinned out a BOX H beef hisself and found the same evidence. That right, Sam?''

''That's right, Capt'n.''

''Morgan, you're being charged with cattle rustlin'. And dependin' on what evidence Butler got, maybe murder too.''

Morgan knew his goose was cooked. The pat hand he thought he had had played out. Morgan went red behind the ears, his mind working at an escape. He could see the only chance open to him. And that was a hope born of clanship. In Morgan's mind no white man would shoot down another white man without a fair fight. He knew his gamble was slim, but the prevailing racial climate gave him hope.

All of a sudden Morgan jabbed spurs to his horse, catapulting out of there. It was so sudden and unexpected that Morgan's horse had taken a dozen jumps before McNelly's pistol came level, aiming directly at Morgan's back.

But a Winchester belched first and a flame leaped out.

A bullet went through the handkerchief pocket of Morgan's suitcoat, ripped into his heart, tore life from him. Morgan's body left the saddle, one foot caught in the stirrup. For some reason his horse trotted over to the jail. A black hand reached out and took hold of the bridle, a voice speaking softly to the unnerved animal.

Ples levered another round in the chamber, looked up the street at McNelly for a reaction. There was none.

McNelly holstered his gun.

Ples turned, wrenched Morgan's foot from the stirrup, tumbling his lifeless body into the street, and walked back inside the jail.

McNelly ran his eyes over Morgan's men, still sitting their saddles in front of him, hang-jawed and spent.

"You men go on about your business," McNelly told them sympathetically. "It's all over and done with."

McNelly and his Rangers walked their horses toward the jail. "Sam," McNelly said to the inspector, "see them beeves get back to their rightful owners."

"Sure will, Capt'n."

"And Sam, you tell Edgemore some of them beeves got more than BAR E on the underside. Brand blottin' is over with. You tell him that from now on any man outside the law will answer."

McNelly sent Armstrong and the rest of the Rangers on down to headquarters at the Exchange Hotel. He went to the jail, to talk to Ples Butler and his men. Ples had already read the telegram from Chief Steele. He said, "Capt'n, you figger that wire was true?"

"It's authentic. Heard last week it was comin' down. Come tomorrow, you boys'll have to do without your guns."

Ples looked at McNelly, a long distasteful look.

"Ain't my doin', Butler," McNelly said. "What law comes down is what I go by."

Ples looked over at Toby, then John, and finally Fate. "I guess that's all she wrote," he said, lifting himself from his chair behind the desk. "Fate, rustle up some travelin' grub."

"I'll send a man over to tend Drake," McNelly said, interrupting the pregnant silence. Then McNelly added a warning: "I don't know about the rest of you men, but was I you, Butler, I'd ride clear out of the country. The reputation you got, you won't live to hear the rooster crow another day without that gun."

McNelly turned away, headed toward the door. "Tomorrow noon, Butler," he said across his shoulder, "have that gun off your hip, or some distance between us."

Hours later Tubac's main street was quiet. The bottom half of the sun had disappeared under the horizon, the top half still throwing out orange rays, casting long shadows over the plank buildings on the east side. The constant sound of music from the Golden Eagle was not to be heard. A mangy dog prowled out of the alley next to the bank. From somewhere behind the hotel facade a mockingbird sang to the wind.

Four men filed out of the jail. Three of them mounted up. The tall, grim-faced, severe man paused at the edge of the boardwalk, swept his eyes up and down both sides of the street dispassionately. "Damn lousy town," he said, more to himself than anybody else, and chuckled, amused.

He mounted up too. No more words were passed. All four men swung their horses away from the hitchrail, headed north. At the edge of town where a man made his own trail, the tall man and the kid swung their horses west. The other two men split off, headed east.

Toby Clark and John Lott, ex–Texas state policemen, rode without side pistols. They rode bare-hipped. Naked as jaybirds. They had both hung up their guns forever. Didn't want to buck the white man's new law.

Ples Butler and Fate Elder rode west. Had government-issued six-shooters slung on their hips, tied down. Ples said he'd wear his gun as long as he drew breath. Fate rode with Ples. He said he didn't have anything else to do.

Chapter Eighteen

Cole knew what to do. One Andalusian was missing. It had been cut out from the horse herd. But he had more than a pretty fair idea who had it. Fact was, he was certain who had it. A long-riding proud warrior such as Black Horse would kill for less of a mount. If any warrior in this bunch had that horse it was Black Horse.

Cole knew it.

The night was steel gray now, dawn coming. The stillness was interrupted by leaves occassionally fluttering in the gentle breeze. A hint of dew was in the air.

Cole was squatting on his haunches in the shadow of a sotol bush a hundred yards downwind, waiting for fires to come to life in Black Horse's camp. Already several warriors had roused themselves and had coaxed dead campfires to life.

Presently at the last of the four campfires, a thin flame took hold, burst to life.

Cole rose to standing, went over to the Andalusian that he had recovered. Speaking softly to the horse, he swung onto the saddle that he had taken from the sentry's horse.

There were at least a dozen warriors moving around, the camps just coming to life. Cole walked his horse up on a small knoll overlooking the campfires, stopped, looking down at the Indians some hundred yards below.

One of the Indians saw him, said something to the others.

Cole kneed the Andalusian around, started riding, flanking the camp, Winchester held across the horse's withers.

Silence broke in the camp, the Indians breaking into a round of muttering in their own tongue, looking at each other, pointing.

And then Cole screamed, war whooped really. A tree-rattling battle cry.

Muttering stopped. Warriors stood dead in their tracks, looking out in awe at the lone man who had boldly ridden in here and issued a challenge to their camp.

Muttering started up again, awed by the bravery of the man.

But a man stretched out next to the last campfire sprang to his feet, grabbed his Winchester.

Black Horse!

Cole knew it was him.

The Andalusian he had tied close by pranced, straining at the picket peg.

Black Horse was at least an inch over six feet. Weighed a good two hundred pounds. He had on blue cavalry pants he'd killed for stuffed inside knee-high leggings, a breech-cloth hanging down over the seat of the pants. He was bare above the waist, showing a bulk of thick muscles at the biceps, and chest. Had a skinning knife on his right hip. A deerskin headband held down long nappy, tight-packed hair. He looked formidable. A fighting man if ever there was one.

Cole triggered off a shot. A spout of dirt leaped up next to Black Horse's feet, stopping him in his tracks. Cole yelped like an Indian again, then wheeled his horse, pointed his

Winchester in the direction the Indians had had the horse herd.

Each warrior's eyes followed the direction Cole's Winchester pointed, and each warrior saw . . .

. . . the horses gone!

Cole drew back on the reins, dug in his heels. The Andalusian backstepped magnificently, spiritedly, then rose up, towering on hind legs. Cole tossed his Winchester aside, as though he was saying "Come on!"

A squat Indian, a Kiowa, looking on impressed, said to Black Horse, "He is of your people, yet he challenges you."

Black Horse spit on the ground contemptuously. "I have no people."

"And he rides the horse you claim," another Indian said.

"He has all our horses," the squat Indian said.

"He challenges you alone, my brother," another Indian, looking to be the oldest of the bunch, pointed out.

Black Horse smiled. "He is no match for me," he said, sweeping his hand over the camp. "Make ready to go. I will kill him quickly. The smell of my woman's wickiup in the tall pines fills my nose," and he pointed to the high peaks of Chinati Mountain. "Wait for me there."

Black Horse threw aside his Winchester, took out running, vaulted over the rump of the other Andalusian, mounted.

Just what Cole wanted.

Cole had figured he had no chance to get the horse back tangling with the whole bunch. His only chance was to have the Andalusian brought to him by drawing out the man who had laid claim to it.

Now looking down the slope, there was the Andalusian in a full-out gallop coming to him as he wanted.

Trouble was, Black Horse was astride that horse.

Cole wheeled his mount, rode away at trail gait.

Black Horse saw the apparent retreat, checked his horse down to a lope.

Suddenly Cole wheeled around, facing Black Horse. Yap-yapping a challenging war whoop as the Indian themselves do, he coaxed Black Horse to follow him. Seeing him coming on, he turned, rode off again, loping lazily across the prairie.

Black Horse was a fighting man if he was anything. Fighting was his existence, a thing he could no more turn his back on than a thirsty man a drink of water.

And this was what Cole was playing to.

Both men knew that only one man would ride away with both horses. The other man's bones would bleach in the high desert sun along with countless others.

Cole slowed his horse, swung east. At a wash deep as a horse's head, he dug in his heels, plunged over the edge, came out on the other side, and wheeled the Andalusian around, luring Black Horse on.

Black Horse came on, riding at a steady gallop, a good clip.

Again Cole swung his mount away, nudged him into a shambling trot this time.

Black Horse took the wash, came out on the other side, his eyes searching for Cole.

But Cole was nowhere in sight.

Black Horse drew up sharply, looking around.

Black Horse saw a field of tumbleweeds windblown up into many waist-high piles. And off to his left stood the horse his adversary had been riding, ground hitched.

Wary now, Black Horse slid from his horse, landed quietly, eyes searching the field of tumbleweeds in front of him.

Which one was his adversary waiting to spring from behind?

Out of the corner of his eye he saw movement.

A horse. Head turned slightly, ears pricked forward at something.

Black Horse smiled cunningly within himself. Leading his

own horse, he circled away quietly, moving stealthily toward the bunch of weeds the horse was watching.

But when he got there, nothing. Only faint moccasin tracks. Leading off toward another clump of tumbleweeds.

He led his horse over to where the other horse was. The horse's head had been reined around deliberately, the rein tied to the saddle skirt, holding the horse's head turned. His ears had pricked naturally at his strange surroundings.

Black Horse smiled, amused. Now he knew his enemy was a man of cunning and ability. A worthy foe.

Cole was watching it all. Lying on his belly in the hot sand behind a giant tumbleweed, looking out at Black Horse through a lattice of twigs.

It was hot, very hot. The sun beat down unmercifully, searing everything and anything. A bead of sweat over Cole's brow broke loose, slid down into his eye. He only squinted against the sting. He dared not move a muscle.

Black Horse gracefully swung aboard his Andalusian, holding on to the reins of the other.

Cole blinked back sweat, doubt starting to creep in.

Black Horse was a man who picked his fighting when the advantage was his. And right now he saw no further profit in continuing to pursue this adversary. He had what he wanted. So he swung his mount and the led horse, heading back to camp and the far upcountry. He could do killings anytime he chose, Black Horse figured. He had the horse. Which was what he wanted.

And Cole knew it.

Looking out from his refuge, Cole knew what had happened was what he feared most: Black Horse would simply take the horse and ride away.

Cole sprang to his feet and yip-yipped the plaintive call of a wounded coyote . . . or dog. To an Indian the mock call of a coward.

Black Horse was no such thing. He stopped. Threw aside

the led horse's reins, wheeled his mount. Slamming heels to the horse's flanks, he dug out, coming at the man who'd called him a coward. He'd let no man live who did that!

Cole stood his ground, feet spread wide.

Like a blur, horse and rider came, charging straight at Cole.

At the last instant Cole leaped aside, and all in the same motion his right hand shot out viciously, open palm slapping across the charging horse's eyes, startling him.

The frightened horse screamed, stopped, digging in its front hoofs, buckjumping at the menace of Cole's hand.

Black Horse came unseated, landing on his belly in a heap.

Blinking away sand and gravel, he gathered himself, sprang to his feet, unsheathing his knife.

Cole had come running, intending to catch Black Horse while he was down. But he was too late. Black Horse had gathered himself from the fall quicker than Cole had expected.

Now Cole drew up short in a fighting stance, ready.

Ten yards separated the two men, both brandishing skinning knives in their right hand. Cole had the one he'd taken from the Indian back in the pass.

Both men crouched low, ready to slash or stab, defend or attack.

Cole circled to his left, searching for an opening, careful not to give one; eyes focused on nothing in particular, alert for movement, any movement at all.

Black Horse circled to his own right, knife held blade up, closing the distance between the two men. Suddenly Black Horse lunged in blade first, shot out a stabbing thrust.

Cole sidestepped the thrust, chopped down at the retreating blade, a wicked chop clanking metal on metal.

Now Cole could see that Black Horse was a bigger man, stronger too. With both men fighting with the knife in their right hand he knew it was simply a test of arm strength. And he'd lose that battle.

So Cole deftly shifted his blade to his left hand.

Now he circled to his left, his right palm forward, ready to deflect the other blade.

Suddenly a foot came out of the sand and a moccasin toe smashed Cole's left wrist, sending his knife sailing into the weeds.

Black Horse grinned knowingly, shifted his blade for the kill, cutting edge sideways for a slashing attack.

Empty-handed now, Cole circled away, hands held high, palms out for parrying.

Black Horse rushed in, slashed left, back right, once upward, then viciously outward. Cole leaped backward wildly out of reach, then ducked left and right, the Indian's blade swishing air.

Cole reached down, picked up a fistful of sand in each hand. Circling away from the blade, he feinted tossing sand into the other man's eyes. Each time Black Horse threw up his left palm to ward off the sand that never came.

Suddenly Cole let fly the sand from his left hand, following it in with his body, grabbing Black Horse's knife hand.

Cole had a death grip on the right wrist. But Black Horse threw a headlock on Cole with his left arm.

Cole twisted around in the headlock, putting his back to the Indian, and with his own left hand reached up, grabbed a handful of hair. Bending low at the waist, pulling with all his might, he snatched Black Horse clear of the ground, somersaulting him over his back, crashing him in the sand.

Cole was running toward him even as Black Horse was tumbling in the sand. Black Horse's body stopped tumbling and a toe smashed his jaw. Black Horse grabbed the foot, heaved up. Cole catapulted back but kept his feet.

Black Horse charged at him, head down.

Cole took the head in the stomach, driving him back into the sand. Black Horse's shoulders came down hard, knocking the wind from Cole.

Black Horse jumped to straddle Cole, wrapping his fingers around Cole's windpipe. Cole's own fingers clawed at his massive arms, trying to remove the steel bands that were shutting off his air.

Cole started to black out; his throat got tight, his eyes felt as if they wanted to pop out.

Cole knew he was no match for the strength of the bigger man.

Almost unconscious, he fumbled getting the thong off his pistol. In what seemed like an eternity to Cole, his gun finally came out of the holster.

He pulled the trigger. The blast was a hollow explosion that rattled around in his head with no meaning whatever.

Black Horse was shocked. His eyes bulged, body stiffened. The muscles of his legs straddling Cole spasmed, went limp. He dropped forward, burying Cole under the hulk of his body.

Cole lay still under the Indian's huge body, catching his wind. Finally, summoning all the strength he had left, he shoved the body off him, rose to sitting, his eyes taking in Black Horse's splendid, mangled body.

Black Horse's side had been shredded, a cavern of torn, powder-burned flesh. Somehow he was not dead yet. He glared at Cole, asked in a firm voice, "Your horses?"

"Fetchin' 'em," Cole answered.

Black Horse's lips trembled, tried to say more but couldn't. He sagged over in the sand. Dead.

Within the hour Cole had got himself ready to travel as best he could. Black Horse was buried in a hastily dug grave. Shallow though it was, Cole hoped the coyotes and wolves wouldn't get at his body.

He was tired, bone tired. He rode out of the valley of Cuesta del Burro riding one Andalusian, leading the other. A long ride ahead of him.

*   *   *

The ranch yard lay still; nothing moved. Two horses over in the far corral cropped grass, switching flies contentedly. From the barn the steady clanking of a blacksmith's hammer on iron pealed out.

Presently Frank Driskill pushed out the screen door, walked leisurely across the yard, heading toward the barn.

At the sound of boot heels, Mike turned, looked up. "Mornin', Pa," he said without emotion. The other man looked up from where he was bent over hammering a nail into a horseshoe. "Morning, Senor Frank."

"Morning, Mike . . . Reyes," Driskill replied. To Mike he added conversationally, "Horse threw a shoe, did he?"

"No sooner than I rode out," Mike answered. "Reyes here will have me in the saddle in no time, though."

"No problemo," Reyes said, dropping the horse's foot to the ground. "She is good as new."

Mike led his horse out of the barn, Frank at his side.

"Jim come in soon as you boys rode out," Frank said casually.

"Tubac still on the map?" asked Mike jokingly.

Frank chuckled halfheartedly. "Just barely, from what Jim tells. Morgan's dead . . . shot down in the street."

"Who done it?"

"State police. Colored feller name Ples Butler."

"Don't seem right, Pa," Mike said sullenly.

"Maybe not," Frank said. "Anyhow . . . coloreds are disarmed as of today. Can't wear guns out in the open no more."

"Lot of good that'll do Morgan," Mike deadpanned.

Mike had stepped a toe into the stirrup, had just reached a hand up to his saddle horn to swing aboard when the clip-clopping of hoofs came to them.

Looking out, they saw a lone rider coming, trailing a led horse.

Mike dropped his foot back to the ground. "That's Cole, ain't it, Pa?" he asked.

"That's him, all right," said Frank. "And he's got the horses!" he added proudly. "I knowed he'd git them!" Then he caught himself. He knew he'd said the wrong thing, showed Mike the wrong side of his thinking.

But Mike had already noticed. His jaws tightened. Temples twitched.

Frank noticed it. And his stomach twisted in knots, apprehensive, worried. They both knew the trouble they had worked so hard to put off was now upon them. Cole's coming was like the plague itself riding in among them.

Cole swung in at the hitchrail in front of the bunkhouse, got down, slapping dust from his jeans. Lifting his eyes, he saw Frank and Mike. He tugged his hat down, started walking toward them.

Mike's eyes held steadily on Cole, watching the desertburnt copper-colored man coming toward him, his mind replaying all that had been said and done, echoing all the whispers he had heard, real and imagined.

Suddenly Mike couldn't take any more. He snapped. He was a man trapped between the shame the community heaped upon him and the respect owed his family.

In his eyes the Driskill name was ruined, disgraced, pulled down from high standing. And it was all Cole's fault.

Mike's hate sprang forth, tearing at his guts.

He threw his reins away from his body, stepped clear of his horse. "Damn you, Cole!" he hollered.

Cole froze in his steps. His eyes found Mike.

"I'm going to kill you!" Mike screamed, his right hand poised at his holster, trembling with rage at what he had to do.

Cole looked at Frank, a confounded, hurt look.

"Don't do it, Mike!" Frank said, looking across his shoulder at Mike. "We can settle this some other way."

Mike ignored the plea, watching Cole.

Cole moved his feet apart, his right hand carelessly at his holster.

Frank's heart leaped in his throat. He knew Mike was fast. But somehow he felt Cole might be faster.

"Get him outa here, Pa!" Mike screamed.

Just then Jim Seely stepped out of the bunkhouse door where the loud talking had gotten his attention. Seely stopped, paralyzed by the sight before him. He knew right away what was happening.

Nora burst through the screen door, running. Across the porch she went. Saw Mike and Cole ready to draw! She stopped in her tracks as if she had been hit in the face with a bucket of cold water. She threw a palm over her mouth, stifling a scream.

Cole took in the scene around him, his mind trying to shut out what was going on. "I fetched the horses," he said aloud to everybody, looking from one face to the next. "That's all I come for. I'll ride."

"People know, Cole!" Mike screamed.

"Let him go, Mike!" Frank yelled. "Let him ride out of here!"

"I can't, Pa," Mike said quietly. "It's too late. They know."

"This don't have to be, Mike," Cole said. "I can ride and y'all won't never hear from me no more."

"But they know," Mike replied.

"Stop gabbing and ride, Cole!" Seely shouted.

"Ain't my choosing," Cole said. "You tell Mike, and I'll ride."

"Mike—" Frank started.

Mike went for his gun.

Cole shot him dead. Beat him to the draw, fair and square.

Nora screamed. Then screamed again.

Frank dropped down on both knees, one fist clenched

against the fates, the other holding his pistol, pointed toward Cole. "My God, boy!" Frank moaned. "Ride! Before I . . ."

Cole blinked stupidly at what he had just done. Frank's voice sobered him. He holstered his pistol, jumped in the saddle, spurred out of there.

Jim Seely was still standing there, dumbfounded, watching Cole's back move away from him.

Days later three men sat around a smokeless campfire of mesquite roots. Night was upon them, but it was still hot, muggy. The country around was broken, wild country, a land where rattlesnakes and coyotes roamed. And Apaches.

The tall severe man, Ples Butler, looked across the fire at the copper-colored fellow who had just ridden in and was now blowing heat from a scalding-hot tin cup of coffee.

"Been in the saddle long?" Ples asked Cole.

"Yeah. Feels like I was born in it," the slim-waisted man said. "Smelled your smoke from up yonder on the ridge. Hoped you wouldn't mind comp'ny."

"Seen our faces too?"

"Yeah."

"Where you headed?" asked Fate Elder, the youngest of the three.

Ples gave his youthful saddle partner a hard look, said quietly, "Man didn't say." Then he added seriously, "Don't you ask."

"West," Cole volunteered anyhow.

The fire crackled and sputtered down to embers, the three men talking, reluctantly at first, then more freely. Each man relating his own story as he wanted it heard. All three knew they didn't have it to do; for this was a land where a man went by any name he chose, and what a man's past was was what he said it was. Unless he was a black man.

215

WILL HENRY

WHO RIDES WITH WYATT

"Some of the best writing the American West can claim!"
—Brian Garfield, Bestselling Author of **Death Wish**

They call Tombstone the Sodom in the Sagebrush. It is a town of smoking guns and raw guts, stage stick-ups and cattle runoffs, blazing shotguns and men bleeding in the streets. Then Wyatt Earp comes to town and pins on a badge. Before he leaves Tombstone, the lean, tall man with ice-blue eyes, a thick mustache and a long-barreled Colt becomes a legend, the greatest gunfighter of all time.

BY THE FIVE-TIME WINNER OF THE GOLDEN SPUR AWARD

___4292-4 $3.99 US/$4.99 CAN

WILL HENRY
JOURNEY TO SHILOH

While the bloody War Between the States is ripping the country apart, Buck Burnet can only pray that the fighting will last until he can earn himself a share of the glory. Together with a ragtag band of youths who call themselves the Concho County Comanches, Buck sets out to drive the damn Yankees out of his beloved Confederacy. But the trail from the plains of Texas to the killing fields of Tennessee is full of danger. Buck and his comrades must fight the uncontrollable fury of nature and the unfathomable treachery of men. And when the brave Rebels finally meet up with their army, they must face the greatest challenge of all: a merciless battle against the forces of Grant and Sherman that will truly prove that war is hell.

_4203-7 $4.50 US/$5.50 CAN

MAX BRAND

"Max Brand is a topnotcher!"
—*The New York Times*

King Charlie. Lord of sagebrush and saddle leather, leader of outlaws and renegades, Charlie rules the wild territory with a fist of iron. But the times are changing, the land is being tamed, and men like Charlie are quickly fading into legend. Before his empire disappears into the sunset, Charlie swears he'll pass his legacy on to only one man: the ornery cuss who can claim it with bullets—or blood.
_4182-0 $4.50 US/$5.50 CAN

Red Devil of the Range. Only two things in this world are worth a damn to young Ever Winton—his Uncle Clay and the mighty Red Pacer, the wildest, most untamable piece of horseflesh in the West. Then in one black hour they are both gone—and Ever knows he has to get them both back. He'll do whatever it takes, even if it costs his life—or somebody else's.
_4122-7 $4.50 US/$5.50 CAN

Dorchester Publishing Co., Inc.
P.O. Box 6640
Wayne, PA 19087-8640

Please add $1.75 for shipping and handling for the first book and $.50 for each book thereafter. NY, NYC, and PA residents, please add appropriate sales tax. No cash, stamps, or C.O.D.s. All orders shipped within 6 weeks via postal service book rate. Canadian orders require $2.00 extra postage and must be paid in U.S. dollars through a U.S. banking facility.

Name_____
Address_____
City_____State_____Zip_____
I have enclosed $_____ in payment for the checked book(s).
Payment <u>must</u> accompany all orders. ❑ Please send a free catalog.

DON'T MISS OTHER
WESTERN ACTION
FROM
LEISURE BOOKS!

Solitude's Lawman by Ray Hogan. To a man like Cole Dagget, eight hundred dollars means a lot of hard hours in the saddle—and just enough to return to Texas, settle down and get married. So when the money is stolen from him in a small-town holdup, there's no way he's going to let the robbers just ride off with it. And he isn't about to wait for the people of Solitude to form a posse.

___4317-3 $3.99 US/$4.99 CAN

Mission to the West by T. V. Olsen. They're a strange trio— the lieutenant, the scout, and the red-haired woman. Part of a peacemaking U.S. Army expedition, they fight their way west, battling the fury of a savage Indian madman. Then they have to survive their trek back through even greater dangers.

___4308-4 $3.99 US/$4.99 CAN

Dorchester Publishing Co., Inc.
P.O. Box 6640
Wayne, PA 19087-8640

Please add $1.75 for shipping and handling for the first book and $.50 for each book thereafter. NY, NYC, and PA residents, please add appropriate sales tax. No cash, stamps, or C.O.D.s. All orders shipped within 6 weeks via postal service book rate. Canadian orders require $2.00 extra postage and must be paid in U.S. dollars through a U.S. banking facility.

Name_____

Address_____

City_____ State_____ Zip_____

I have enclosed $_____ in payment for the checked book(s).

Payment <u>must</u> accompany all orders. ☐ Please send a free catalog.

BONNER'S STALLION
T. V. OLSEN

Winner of the Golden Spur Award

Bonner's life is the kind that makes a man hard, makes him love the high country, and makes him fear nothing but being limited by another man's fenceposts. Suddenly it looks as if his life is going to get even harder. He has already lost his woman. Now he is about to lose his son and his mountain ranch to a rich and powerful enemy—a man who hates to see any living thing breathing free. That is when El Diablo Rojo, the feared and hated rogue stallion, comes back into Bonner's life. He and Bonner have one thing in common...they are survivors.

___4276-2 $4.50 US/$5.50 CAN

BREAK THE YOUNG LAND

T. V. OLSEN

Winner of the Golden Spur Award

Borg Vikstrom and his fellow Norwegian farmers are captivated when they see freedom's beacon shining from the untamed prairies near a Kansas town called Liberty. In order to stake their claim for the American dream they will risk their lives and cross an angry ocean. But in the cattle barons' kingdom, sodbusters seldom get a second chance...before being plowed under. With a power-hungry politico ready to ignite a bloody range-war, it is all the stalwart emigrant can do to keep the peace...and dodge the price that has been tacked on his head.

_4226-6 $4.50 US/$5.50 CAN